FLIGHT OF THE WHITE WOLF

FLIGHT OF THE WHITE WOLF

by Mel Ellis

SCHOLASTIC INC.
New York Toronto London Auckland Sydney

THE WOLF in this story is fashioned after Kepa, an animal belonging to Lucille and Orin Benson of Eagle, Wisconsin. Otherwise, all characters in this book are fictitious, and any resemblance to actual persons, living or dead, is purely coincidental.

ISBN 0-590-42053-4

Published by Scholastic Inc., 730 Broadway, New York, NY 10003, by arrangement with Henry Holt and Company, Inc. APPLE PAPERBACKS is a registered trademark of Scholastic Inc.

12 11 10 9 8 7 6 5 4 3 2 1 10 8 9/8 0 1 2 3/9

Printed in the U.S.A. 01

TO KEPA

. . . the big white wolf who survived for twenty-one days in the Kettle Moraine Forest almost within the shadows of the Milwaukee, Wisconsin, skyline. True friend of Lucille and Orin Benson, who raised him from a pup to a magnificent animal, Kepa, who had strayed, finally came to a trap set for foxes and that is where they found him. He still lives — does Kepa — faithful to Orin and loving Lucille, but neither fawning nor subservient to either. I met him, at his home near Eagle, when he was a frolicking pup. Watched him mature and helped hunt him when he had strayed. He taught me that among wolves there is such dignity as is only sometimes found among men.

1

THE WOLF LAY at the end of a long, strong tether watching the dog. Off to one side, and almost hidden by the bending boughs of an oak hung with the auburn leaves of autumn, a boy watched both of them.

The dog, a boxer only a shade lighter than the oak leaves, was taunting the wolf with his eyes and ears and teeth and every bristling hair.

If the wolf, almost white against the coppery background of frostbitten foliage, was concerned, he was careful not to show it. He was stretched out, sharp muzzle down on his forepaws. His eyes were the merest slits, and only the tip of his tongue moved as, from time to time, he moistened his nose so the scent of the dog would come more sharply through the nerve endings to his brain.

The boy, of course, knew about them, about how the wolf hated the dog with every fiber of his wild beginnings. And the boy knew too how the dog hated the wolf, and how he did all such things as the runners, dogs and wolves, will do to aggravate one another.

It was an explosive situation. The wolf, always either tethered or kenneled, had to watch while the dog roamed freely, leaving his mark on tree, bush, and post in an invisible but insulting ring.

But wolves can wait. They are past masters at patience, else they would long have expired from this earth, because without a bred-in discipline, they would never have learned to follow caribou herds until one sickened, never stayed days on a deer's trail until one tired, nor learned to lay at a den entrance for long hours to get such a small mouthful as one ground squirrel.

The boy stepped from beneath the boughs of the great oak, and the wolf's head came up and his ears came forward. The boxer turned too, but if there was anything in his demean-

or, or any look on his pushed-in face, it was only one of disdain, because the dog — a perfect show animal and only kept for breeding purposes — had come, in some inexplicable manner, to understand how valuable he was.

"Beat it, Bo," the boy said, addressing the dog.

But the dog refused to move off. So reaching as though to pick up a stone, the boy made a flinging motion, but he knew better than to think the dog would run off yipping, as might some lesser canine. Instead Bo turned, and with head held high, made a deliberate exit from the scene, bringing each paw high, as he had learned to do in the show ring from which he usually emerged winner of another blue ribbon.

The boy, Russet Clagg, went over to where the wolf lay and dropped to his knees beside him. The wolf whimpered, but if you were not listening for it, you might have thought it was only one small twig in the oak rubbing gently against another to produce a brief, mouselike sound.

"Don't let him get to you, Gray," the boy said, lifting the wolf's head to his lap. The tip of the wolf's tongue showed briefly as though in answer. "You could whip a half-dozen like him, given the chance. Only, what would it get you?" the boy asked. Again the pink tip of the wolf's tongue appeared.

The boy sat, running his hands roughly through the wolf's coat of coarse hairs and then, getting up, started toward the house which squatted comfortably in another oak grove which spread trees along the opposite side of the drive, across from where the wolf was tethered.

Russ's home was part of a scattered complex of buildings, which together combined to be one of the largest and most modern training and boarding kennels for dogs in Wisconsin.

The main kennel, with scores of concrete runs and tiled cubicles, was across the County Trunk highway, so the noise of the barking dogs would never intrude too insistently upon anyone trying to rest in the house.

The whole of it, house and kennels and numerous outbuildings for sheltering food supplies and game birds kept to train dogs, was in the heart of a southern Wisconsin state forest, the Kettle Moraine — such a lush place of trees as is rarely found in agricultural country during these days of intensive farming.

Russ smelled baking bread even before he opened the kitchen door. Though the Claggs might drive the latest jeeps and pleasure cars, watch color television, or entertain on silver service, his mother had never been able to give up baking her own bread. His mouth watered, as it always did, and he hurried a little now, hoping it was out of the oven and he might have a piece.

Opening the door and going in, he saw that his father, a lean and angular man with long limbs and a hard middle, was already sampling the bread. His mother, a small dark woman of high color, with what seemed a perpetual half-smile on her lips, was just putting a fresh batch of smoothly rounded dough loaves into the oven, from which the first crisp bread had just been removed.

"So you smelled it too," his mother said, closing the oven door and turning to him.

He hadn't really, not until he had gotten near the house, but he nodded that he had because he knew it gave her pleasure to think so, and then he watched while she cut him a thick slice.

He was about to take a bite of the bread which was running golden with butter, when he remembered why he had come to the house. Turning to his father, he said:

"That Bo! He's driving Gray crazy. Isn't there some way we can confine him?"

As soon as it was out, he knew he shouldn't have asked it. Bo could not stand confinement. He languished. His appetite disappeared. He thinned out, became stringy. His duties as a stud dog, as a breeding animal, were interfered with. He could not be shown, exhibited. So, of all the dogs, he was the one permitted the run of the grounds, and he was enough of a braggart to make his privileged status clear to every tethered or caged thing.

Cal Clagg only shrugged. He knew about the boy's concern for the wolf's feelings, but he also could count, and whereas the wolf hadn't added a dollar to the credit side of the kennel's ledger, the boxer was worth thousands.

Russ didn't pursue the subject, but addressed himself to the piece of homemade bread. The butter ran down his chin.

He knew he shouldn't have brought up the subject in the first place. It had been childlike, and since his parents always treated him with as much respect as they might another adult, there was no reason for him to come whimpering.

In the kennel, there was always the occasional prima donna among the dogs, but never among the boys and men entrusted with the development, feeding, and care of their charges. It was a Clagg rule to sort out the dogs so each trainer who worked at the kennel — so even Cal Clagg and even Russ — had his own allotment of animals, and unless you went looking for advice, there was no interference.

Bo was his father's responsibility. The wolf, over the years, had come to belong to Russ. So long as there was no physical confrontation, Russ had no right to seek curtailment of Bo's liberties and, likewise, his father never interfered so far as the wolf was concerned.

That was why Cal didn't bother to answer his son's complaint, and that was why Russ never really expected to get an answer.

They both finished the bread and started toward the door together. Just as Cal Clagg put his hand to the latch, an ominous growl came through the open window. In one quick movement, he threw the door open and stepped out onto the porch. Russ followed, and both men were just in time to see the wolf hit the end of his tether in what must have been a fast sprint, and a wild, almost winging leap.

They saw the great white animal hang in midair as the leash checked him. Then they knew that either the swivel or snap had parted, because Gray went catapulting forward, end over end, sending the first fallen leaves flying.

The somewhat sedentary boxer turned as though to flee, but he must have known that already, even before the wolf got to him, there was no help. He must have realized, in that split instant when the tiny piece of metal snapped, that his life had been broken too. So he turned, champion that he was, to meet the wolf and to go down fighting.

Father and son had gotten down the steps and off the porch when the pair closed. The boxer snarled, but the wolf got on with the killing quietly. With one bite he broke a front leg, and Bo went down. Instantly his jaws, huge enough to crack a caribou's thigh bone for the sweet marrow in it, closed over the boxer's throat.

Deeper he dug then, always chomping, until he felt the spurt of blood from the jugular. Then, with blood staining his white face and almost blinding him, he backed away and realized, perhaps for the first time, that he was free. He turned at once and loped for the oaks and the slope which ran thick with prickly ash and all manner of small trees such as grow on the edge areas of pine forests.

Cal and Russ ran to Bo, but even as they knelt beside the twitching body, they knew life had left it.

"The wolf!" Cal said quietly. "The wolf. We've got to get him!"

Russ looked up in time to see Gray come to the top of the small ridge, one of several which angled down to the small valley floor on which the kennel complex stood. He got up, and in what he hoped was a quiet and reassuring manner, called: "Gray. Here. Come, Gray. Gray."

The wolf neither fled nor came back down the ridge, but only stood at the summit, a huge animal sloping from a high, broad brow down to wide powerful shoulders and narrowing flanks which seemed set like springs always ready to release their power.

"Gray," the boy said the name quietly, just loud enough for the wolf to hear, and then he started up the slope through the prickly ash, among the little trees, which were a leafy fringe to the pine forest, until he was within twenty feet of the animal. Then, Gray turned and ran.

"Be careful," he heard his father say, but he wasn't afraid of the wolf, but only afraid that Gray might keep running.

When Russ topped out on the ridge the wolf was nowhere in sight, but he knew what trail he would likely take, and followed it among the pines, down now until he came to the wide place in Red Cherry Creek, and there was Gray's track — wide across as a man's hand in the mud.

The boy sloshed across the creek and saw where Gray had left drops of water on a clump of cattails, on the hazel brush, on the game trail which started up the side of another ridge.

Russ felt inclined to run, but he knew haste might make Gray apprehensive. He felt the wolf was too intelligent to panic, but if he pushed too fast the wolf might line out, take a straightaway course, and run it hard.

So he moved up the game trail at a moderate pace, and sometimes he gave the small, sharp whistle the wolf knew, and sometimes he spoke the animal's name softly. Once he thought he glimpsed Gray among the thickening trees, and then he waited, hoping the animal would come to him. When he didn't, he moved on, always looking for a sign so he might know he was still on the trail.

For a while there were occasional drops of water, and once there was a tiny tuft of grayish-white hair in a small clearing where brambles struggled for survival, but then there was nothing, and he couldn't know for sure if he was on the wolf's trail or if he had lost it.

But, if he guessed rightly, the wolf would be the one to maintain contact. If he knew his wolf, as he thought he did, Gray would never go so far as to be out of smelling range. Or if he did, he would backtrack until he was satisfied that he, Russ, was still in the forest with him.

Even the wild wolves, those who never crossed the trails of men, preferred familiar things, though these might only be an old den, a comfortable copse, a certain scent post, a pile of rocks — and in all this world there was, as of this moment, perhaps no stronger attachment, nor any more familiar thing for Gray than the boy.

So finally, when he could not bring the wolf in view, the boy stopped and sat on a log. From time to time he whistled softly, and several times he left the log to circle on the wind so the wolf would have to circle too if he were to keep him within scent range. In this way he hoped to get a glimpse of him.

But it is conceivable that the wolf had some understanding of this thing he had done in killing the boxer dog. As a wolf, he had not been exempted from the reward and punishment code with which humans govern all lesser life. And now, having been punished before for first killing a duck, second killing a chicken, and third threatening to kill a snappish dachshund, perhaps he understood the wrong he had done.

So perhaps that is why he stayed out ahead, or perhaps it was because all his life he had yearned to be free, since nothing the boy or the man or even the solicitous woman could do for him was enough to compensate for the cage or the leash which forever held him prisoner.

The boy left the log and walked again. He crossed the same creek twice, because it curled almost back on itself in making its torturous trek through the forest. Each time, on examining the shorelines, he found Gray's tracks. Encouraged, he continued until he was in a dense section of forest near which there were but few buildings, all of which had been abandoned when the state acquired the property to add to its forest.

Here he decided to wait, and under the thick pines evening came early; and then if there hadn't been starlight, he wouldn't have seen the wolf come quietly and stretch out on the pine needles not twenty feet away.

Russ talked to Gray then, but he did not get up and try to approach him. He spoke quietly with neither fear nor anger or any emotion which might alienate the wolf. When Gray showed no sign of wanting to come closer, he decided it would be useless to try to capture him in darkness, and, taking off his sweater, made a pillow, and stretched out for the night.

Several times during the night he awakened and, lifting to an elbow, waited for his eyes to adjust themselves. Then, gradually, the silhouette of the white wolf would come into focus, and he would lie back down and go to sleep.

In the morning he got up, stretched, and talked softly to Gray, who now lay stretched full-length where he had been curled all night. But now he tried to approach the animal and, taking off his belt, meant to use it for a short leash, if Gray would give him permission.

But it didn't work. Though he approached the wolf diagonally, as if he only intended on walking past, Gray moved out when he came within ten feet. He tried again and again, and discovered that the critical distance was almost exactly ten feet. The wolf had no intention of permitting him to move closer.

So he would have to find some other way, and meanwhile he might feel better if he found something to eat. Well, there were apples, and he knew of the abandoned orchard near the crumbling buildings, so he went there for breakfast and Gray followed along.

Then he began a gradual drift back toward home, hoping if he brought the wolf near enough to familiar places, the animal might be content to come in. Gray followed along dutifully, but even before they came up on the ridge from which they could look down on the kennels, the wolf showed signs of apprehension.

"Easy, Gray. Easy," the boy tried to soothe the wolf.

But the wolf would not be comforted. He refused to follow up the ridge and remained in the cut below. Russ went up the ridge and looked down. There were an uncommonly large number of cars about the place. They were parked in the drive by the house and across the road in the parking lot reserved for customers. There were some sheriff vehicles and two state police cars, and then it occurred to the boy that the word was out that the wolf was on the loose, and these men had come to hunt him.

He looked back to where Gray waited. Then he looked back toward his home, and he surmised that one or another of the kennel employees had spread the word about the wolf, because he knew his parents would have tried quietly, on their own, to get the animal back. Then, even as he watched, three men, all carrying guns, crossed the road.

He didn't wait but hurried down the ridge, and taking the game trail over which he had previously pursued the wolf, trotted toward denser cover.

Well, he thought, if they were coming with guns to get the wolf, they would have to work at it, and he struck out across the creek to come at last to where he'd slept the night before. In this dense stand of pines he made himself comfortable with his back against a log and waited, and always the wolf stayed close by.

The day droned along to the monotonous whirr and rustle of insects. Twice he walked back as far as one elbow of the creek for a drink, and once he went to an edge area where there were brambles and stripped a pint of dried berries from the bushes for his stomach.

But he could think of no plan of action, of no way out of this predicament for the wolf, so long as he couldn't get his belt looped through the collar to bring Gray safely past anyone who might be gunning for him.

So he must wait or abandon the animal. By night he was hungry enough to experience a little pain, and he knew that whatever else, he must eat.

So, in the first darkness, he moved out to the edge of the forest and, staying in the shadow, moved in the direction of the kennels. But he hadn't gone a half-mile when he heard voices, and then along the roadway saw the bright stab of flashlights. So he cut back among the trees and saw Gray run out and disappear ahead of him.

It wasn't until he was safely back among the trees that the wolf rejoined him. Then the two of them lay down, and Russ realized he would have to go another night without food.

In the morning he moved again until he was back under the gnarled limbs of the old abandoned orchard, but he knew his stomach could not long tolerate such fare, so he wondered about snaring a rabbit.

The wolf apparently was not yet suffering from hunger. Like most wild carnivores, Gray could fast for days. He still moved easily and strongly through the forest, always a reasonable distance from the boy. Then, at noon, they came to the marsh where there might be rabbits.

Almost at once the wolf's head went up and he thrust his muzzle forward so the boy knew that some scent line, like an invisible rope, was pulling at Gray.

He followed along, hoping it was a cottontail and the wolf might catch it. But where a trail came down out of the forest the wolf hesitated, reluctant to advance. The boy went around him, and he saw the bait of meat hanging by a thin rope from the branches of an alder bush.

He knew at once. It was a trap! Carefully he advanced, and then he saw the ill-concealed trap beneath the leaves and, taking a stick, he triggered it. Then he pulled the bait, a couple pounds of half-raw beef, from the alders and walked back from the marsh edge until he was once again beneath the trees.

He wondered if the trap had been set for the wolf, or if some fox hunter had placed it there. There were no wild wolves in the Kettle Moraine, of course, nor even any coyotes in that far southern part of the state.

Back under the trees he sat to look at the meat. It was unsavory looking, and was blue along the edges, and apparently on the verge of becoming tainted. Nevertheless, he threw the wolf half of it, and then, sitting with his back against the trunk of a tree, slowly ate the other half.

His stomach, on the verge of revolt, finally settled down to accept the meat. When he'd managed to down the last scrap, his stomach came to terms with the food, and he could hear it gurgle as juices went to work to break down the sinews of beef so they might be converted into strength.

After eating he rested, and once more then, headed for the creek so they could drink. Halfway to water the wolf stopped, and when he did the boy dropped to his knees to listen.

It was a while before he heard voices, and when he did, he crawled into the hazel brush and, lying there, watched while the wolf retreated. The hunting party passed within a hundred yards of where he lay hidden. Now he knew this might be a hunt to death for Gray, unless he found some way of getting him to the safety of the kennels, or of getting him completely out of this country into some other part of the state.

2

FOR TWO DAYS they dodged posses. They were difficult days spent hiding in the thickest part of the forest, and they were difficult nights because Russ's sleep became a hideous time of wild nightmares. He ate apples and berries and found one wild plum tree with fruit. There was one rabbit, chased into a rock pile, which he dug out, and after peeling off its fur coat, cooked it over a small, cautious fire.

Then on the fourth night, with the forest literally alive with search parties, they took to a high ledge, and it was here the searchers finally cornered them.

The line of marchers had come in darkness to a clearing made by a Big Burn. From their vantage point on the cliff above the pines, both fugitives could see the frantic flashing of lights as the posse cleared the trees and started up the coulee which fire had gutted some years before.

"Gray, we've got to get out of here!"

More and more, of late, the boy had taken to talking to the wolf. Perhaps it was only to hear the sound of his own voice and to get whatever encouragement there might be in that. Or perhaps it was because, in this predicament, they had become closer than they had ever been during their seven years together — even though the wolf wouldn't let him come close, wouldn't let him touch him.

Their ledge fronted on a tiny cave where the boy had sought shelter. Though Gray would not enter the cave, he had stood guard outside it. But the boy had known it was only a matter of time before someone remembered the ledge and the cave, and the hunt would take that direction.

Intermittent rain, sometimes turning to sleet, had been a factor in choosing this hideout. Soaked through and shivering uncontrollably, he had at last climbed the ledge to crawl into the cave and, curling up, hoped body heat would dry his clothing.

Now, sounds emanating from the posse became louder as the lights below began to group. The men apparently were going to talk it over before sweeping up the coulee for an assault on the ledge.

Russ couldn't help wondering why there were so many posses, and why they should go to the trouble of hunting at night. Mostly they had been dodging search parties during daylight, and their nights had usually been uninterrupted.

It must have been the lamb. Gray, finally hungry beyond reason, had jumped a lamb at dusk, and every sheep in that whole big flock had gone blathering straight back toward the farm. He had tried to call the wolf off, but Gray hadn't left until dogs were barking and men were running and shouting.

Russ looked over to where Gray was an indistinct white fresco of a wolf painted against a clump of spruce. In the dark he couldn't pick out details, but he knew Gray would be alert with ears erect and eyes narrowed. Every hair would be bristling with apprehension, and just the tip of the pink tongue would be showing, the way it always did when the wolf was perturbed.

Back home they had been such a companionable pair, but by now Russ had come to understand how here in the forest, on the wolf's own ground, theirs might be a somewhat uneasy truce.

If only he might have gotten his belt through the wolf's collar, all this might have been avoided. As it was, their predicament was steadily worsening, and he was old enough — fifteen — to realize they couldn't run forever. Yet, even had Gray submitted, Russ wondered if he *wanted* to walk the wolf back to the kennels and, handing him over, say: "Well, here he is! And now, what are you going to do with him?"

For Russ there would have been no problem had they been in Wisconsin's north woods, where it is still wild enough for a wolf to make his way. There, perhaps, he could have, in good conscience, simply abandoned the animal.

But here! Even from where the pair crouched, they could see the luminous sky which marked the millions of lights of Milwaukee. And, stringing out in every direction from Milwaukee, roads were laced like a network of vines, with suburbs and villages clustering thick as leaves. Except for the narrow, thirty-mile-long slash of forest in which they were hiding, the country around was so thickly populated even a snake might have trouble threading its way through without being detected. Gray could never make it (Russ was convinced) on his own — not anywhere in southeastern Wisconsin.

The men in the coulee below had lighted a fire and were crowding around it. Russ shivered violently. The sleet had stopped. It was misting, and moisture beaded like ice drops on the wool of his sweater, in his tousled hair.

His Mukwonago Union High School sweater with lettering (in recognition of his cross-country triumphs) was warm, but he had on thin trousers and no hat nor any gloves. He did have on low, leather bird-shooter boots, and at least they were a comfort on the rugged terrain.

There were some sounds of merriment below, and Russ suspected someone was passing around a bottle. That would slow them down, but it would also make them more dangerous.

So far as the wolf was concerned, Russ knew his fate was sealed if anyone got close enough to get Gray in his sight. Though he couldn't see the members of the posse, he knew that every man and boy in it carried a gun. He also knew that each was anxious to use it, because whoever could claim the big white wolf would be the local hero.

Gray shifted position on the ledge. Russ

knew the wolf was getting nervous. The sound of voices, the flashing of lights were wearing the thin thread of domesticity even thinner, and Russ knew the wolf was on the verge of spooking and making a run for it.

Russ knew about wolves. He had not only lived with this one for seven years, he had made a study of them. When it came to wolves, few adults were as knowledgeable.

It had started when he was eight and Gray had come — a snarling, angry little bundle of gray fur, snatched out of a northwood's den, from the breast of his dead mother.

Russet's father had brought the pup home from the kennels across the road. "We'll let him live with us until he thinks he's people," he had said, "otherwise there's no hope for him."

The wolf hadn't been Clagg's idea originally. Gray had been the gift of a friend, but once Cal had the pup, he saw the possibility of working him into the dog act he took to sport shows across the country.

In a kennel as large as Clagg's, names are always at a premium, so it seemed most natural to call him Gray. But that was before he turned white and grew to be a 135-pound giant of his kind.

Though the little wolf never got to think

of himself as people, he gradually turned tolerant and stayed that way until coming to maturity at the age of three.

Then quite suddenly, and for no apparent reason, he wouldn't let anyone except Russet touch him. Those who tried felt his fangs. It was always only a warning. He'd take a hand or an arm between his jaws and close down, though never with enough pressure to break the skin.

Russ was not fooled by the wolf's faithfulness to him. He suspected that Gray regarded him as a younger and not quite capable member of his pack. Hadn't they shared the same bed? Eaten together on the stoop? Roamed the hills? Played? Quarreled? Been cold and warm and happy and sad together?

Down in the coulee, men were stamping out the fire. Sparks flew as they scattered embers with their boots. The flashlights came on and began again cutting the darkness with erratic knife-slashes of light.

Russ looked to Gray. During their seven years together they had learned to cue on each other. Now it was time. The line had formed and they *were* coming toward the cliff.

Russ wished the wolf had been better trained. But his father had given up training the animal, and Gray had been moved to a kennel and run adjoining the garage. After maturity he had never been allowed out except on a leash, and of the thousands of people and hundreds of dogs to cross his path, he never showed any real animosity toward any except the big boxer and the little dachshund he had threatened to kill for pestering him.

But now he was the hunted, because the countryside had been alerted, and a wolf hunt might even take precedence over the war, political campaigns, the riots in the streets. . . . Russ sensed this and was driven by the ferocity of the searchers and their obvious determination to destroy the wolf.

Even so, there were times when Russ felt his job was to try to take Gray in to stand trial for his lapse of civility. But, having killed, would he ever again be permitted outside a cage, even on leash? Having usurped man-made rules, wouldn't man, in his abysmal ignorance of the natural law which governed wolves and all the wild ones, demand a life of absolute servility? Would anyone ever be kind to him again?

People! Russ was sure most didn't know anything about wolves. They only remembered that it was a wolf which ate Red Riding Hood's grandmother. They never knew, in fact, that the wolf was a timid creature, tuned only to fight such natural wild enemies as might threaten it.

"Just keeping captive wolves human-oriented," Cal Clagg had said, "takes devotion and thousands of hours of attention on the part of man. Neglect a wolf for a week, a month, two months, and the animal quickly returns to a wild state of mind."

Well, he'd never take the wolf in now, he told himself. There could be only one way, and that was north. Somehow, he didn't know now, but in some manner he would have to find a way to take Gray back to the wild land from which he'd come, back to that kind of country where once a man had plucked him from a dim den while still a pup.

Now the line of men with guns had formed and was moving forward. Russ heard Gray get to his feet. He knew the animal was trembling with apprehension. He knew wolves, though ready to attack even grizzly bears to protect their young, had such an innate fear of man that some had been known to die of shock at the touch of a trapper's hand.

But now there was no more time to think

on it. Russ could hear Gray breathing as both ends of the long line of lights began to make their circle to surround the escarpment. They'd have to get out now. In another minute it would be too late, and the searchers would have encircled them.

"Okay, Gray," Russ whispered.

The wolf turned, and staying close to the ground, started down the precipitious backside of the cliff. The boy followed carefully lest he start rocks rolling and alert members of the posse to their presence.

The forward line of men was so close now that Russ could hear them shouting instructions and encouragement to each other. They were urging the end men to hurry, to close the trap.

"If he's up there we've got to get all the way around or he'll squeeze out," Russ heard a man shout.

The boy came to the bottom of the cliff just as the twin pincers of encirclement moved around the base of the bluff. He looked ahead and got a fleeting glimpse of white as the wolf bolted out of the fire-gutted coulee into a thick stand of pines.

Gray had made it, but the boy knew now the trap had closed on him. If he ran, someone's light would be certain to spot him out, and it is conceivable that a trigger-happy hunter might shoot him by mistake.

He dropped to his knees and crawled, and when he came to a dry creek bed which veined the coulee, he rolled into it and lay still. Almost at once lights roamed over the creek bed. He heard the squish of boots in wet grass, the sound of heels on stone, the rasp of corduroy and leather. Now the boys and men were silent because they supposed, they hoped their quarry was at bay.

Well, if they found Russ, Gray would still be free. But for how long? Alone, what chance would he have? How could he ever break out of the web? And, should he get out to more rural areas, it would only be a matter of time before someone out there sighted him and then the posses would be formed again. The cry "WOLF!" would echo from town to town, and someday, somewhere, he'd be cornered, and a shot would come like the sharp slap of leather against leather, and then the big white wolf would be dead.

A boot came down so close to Russet's head he could see the leather laces. He tried to melt right into the creek bottom, to become a part of the earth.

Above, lights crissed and crossed, and

low voices, one guiding on the other, were so close he could even hear the breathing.

Russ felt the toe of a boot against his leg. He braced waiting for the instant of discovery. Then the other boot went over the top, just grazing him, and was put down and the searcher passed on.

Sounds around were diminishing. He dared to raise his head. The line had passed over him and was on its way to the cliff. Still he lay quiet, not daring to move. It wasn't until he heard the searchers start small rock slides as they assaulted the sides of the cliff that he began to crawl toward the protection of the pines.

"Watch out now! He's likely to make a break for it!" someone was shouting.

Russ got to his feet and began running. Then, the wet needles of the red pines slapped him in the face. He burst through the young growth and then, on the cushioned forest floor, he moved away until the sounds of pursuit came only intermittently. He dropped and the odor of pine needles was a sharp stimulant, and the feel of the cool ground was as welcome as a swim on a hot August day. For a while he breathed hard. Then he began to relax and shortly he slept.

3

A SHAFT OF SUNLIGHT through the pines awakened him. He lay without moving, rolling his eyes for some sign of danger. A movement in the low branches caught his attention. It was a chickadee turning its head from side to side with curiosity because a man was sleeping on its forest floor. Slowly, then, Russ turned his head and, when he did, it was to look straight into the eyes of Gray.

The wolf's tongue was lolling. His eyes were wide, the way he held them when he was pleased with himself and the world and there was no enemy to contemplate.

Russet sat up. Muscles in his legs were

sore. He rubbed them gently, and then ran a hand through his tousled hair.

"Bet I look like something the cat dragged in," he said quietly to Gray.

Like a big dog, the wolf turned his head from side to side. Russ looked at him intently. "You're sure in a good mood. You going to let me touch you today?"

As if in reply the wolf made the playful gesture of dropping to his forepaws which was the signal for a romp. Russ took the cue, but when he got to his feet and started toward Gray, the wolf's jaws closed, his eyes narrowed, and he walked off to one side.

"Okay, if that's the way you want it. But, tell me, what's for breakfast?"

Again, the white wolf opened his jaws and let his tongue loll and the elliptical eyes opened wider.

During the four days they had eaten but little. What they'd had, hadn't been nearly enough. The wolf looked lank, and though Russ hadn't lost any weight, he could feel the emptiness in his stomach, and it sometimes hurt as if a hot stone had been dropped there.

"There's a creek near here," the boy said to the wolf. "Let's go get a drink and wash up."

The day promised to be warm, a relief after the rain which had turned fitfully at times into sleet. The creek was running brim full, and there were leaves from a bank birch like little golden boats sailing on the current.

Before stretching out to drink, Russ looked at Gray. The wolf gave no sign of danger in the vicinity, so he stretched out on his stomach and lowered his head to the water. Before he put his mouth to the stream, he got a good look at himself and was surprised to see that his face and hair were mud-streaked from lying in the dry wash the night before.

The water was cold and had a sweet taste of the earth. After he'd sucked enough to satisfy his thirst, he dunked his head under. He lifted it dripping and scrubbed with his hands, dunked again, and then shook his head so the water flew. Finding a pine cone he raked it through his hair, straightening the curls and snarls flat to his head. Then he took another look at himself and, turning to the wolf, asked: "Better? Is that better?"

The wolf looked at him quizzically. Russ laughed. "Might do you good," he said. "You're starting to smell."

But the frivolous mood was not enough to sustain them because they were hungry, and so the boy moved out.

The wolf, instead of staying at heel, ranged out ahead and cast back and forth like a pointing dog trying the air.

They made a strange pair. Small for fifteen, Russ weighed little more than the wolf, though he was a thong of a boy, rawhide tough from cross-country running and doing a man's work at the kennels. His normally brown hair had turned almost white in the summer sun, and his face was brown as the boots he wore. He walked with an easy stride and covered ground almost as effortlessly as did Gray.

Russ knew the country well, and when the terrain began to slope downward, he was aware that they were coming to the edge of a large marsh. He watched the wolf for signs, and went more carefully when Gray put his ears far forward and dropped from a high-stepping trot to a low slink.

Russ interpreted the maneuver as signifying food ahead. If there had been danger, Gray would have stopped, put his ears back, and then turned aside or retreated.

They broke quietly from among the trees just as a hen pheasant settled into the brown marsh grass fifty feet ahead. The boy crouched when Gray did. Together they remained motionless watching a file of pheasants take off from a cornfield where they'd been feeding, to fly back to the marsh.

Two more hens and one brilliant cock landed where they'd seen the first hen dump down. They waited until there were no more birds in the air, and then Russ looked to where Gray was crawling on his belly toward the birds.

He hadn't seen the wolf stalk anything since the animal had been a pup. But during Gray's formative years, he had played at the game incessantly. Leaves, a stick, a glove, an old shoe — anything had been fair game, and he would slither toward the hunted object, ending the stalk with a mighty leap of triumph.

Now Gray had the scent of pheasant hot and true in his nostrils. Russ could tell that much from his absolute concentration. Gray was going like a magnet to where the birds had landed, as if he had no choice except to follow the scent line into the flock.

The maneuver might have worked with quail, Hungarian partridge, sharptail grouse, or even woodcock or jacksnipe. But what Gray didn't know, and the boy did, was that pheasants won't hold, but will run out ahead long before the wolf got close enough to leap in for the kill.

So Russ quickly circled so they had the birds between them. Gray stopped. He didn't understand.

When the wolf resumed his stalk, Russ took a few steps forward as though to close the trap. Again Gray paused, obviously perturbed that the boy should show himself to the pheasants and perhaps frighten them into flight.

Then, as though from some instinctive well of antiquity, the wolf got the idea. It was a trick as old as wolves were, the ruse of distracting a caribou or deer or hare so the hidden member of the hunting team could crawl close enough to kill. Even coyotes knew the trick and used it. Foxes too were adept at this deception. Now Russ was just another wolf doing his part as a member of the pack.

But the cock spotted the wolf when death was an instant away and lifted cackling an alarm. A hen followed in the rooster's flight pattern, but the third hen made the mistake of flying toward the trees directly over Gray's head.

As though catapulted into the air by strong springs, the wolf leaped. Feathers showered about. The hen made a piping sound, then its life gurgled away with the blood in its throat. Gray stretched on the grass, the hen beneath his forepaws, shaking his head to rid himself of the feathers which clung wetly to his flews.

In the excitement of the kill, Russ forgot himself and ran forward. A look from the wolf warned him back. He stood waiting and the wolf was motionless; the only thing that moved on the edge of that brown marsh were oak leaves on a bough and the quivering wing feathers of the dying bird.

When at last the hen lay quiet, Gray got up and, picking up his prey, turned from the boy and went at a fast trot for the trees. Russ started to follow, but he went only as far as the forest fringe. There he sat to ponder on their predicament, which could only deteriorate until such time as he had no strength left to care for the wolf, and the wolf had no strength left to care for himself. They couldn't, it now seemed obvious, continue to live on the very fringes of a large city, in this thirty-mile slash of state forest, and expect to survive. Even if they were fortunate enough to escape being killed or captured, here they would starve.

The alternative was to turn themselves in. But how, when the wolf refused to go?

Maybe, the boy thought, it would be the wise thing to simply bring the wolf within range of the guns and have it over with.

Dogs sometimes had to be disposed of. Hadn't he helped put the needle of death to more than should have been his share during so short a life?

This is no time for sentimentality, he thought. In fact, sentimentality should never get in the way of the man-animal relationship. Trouble was, it did. And you couldn't help it. And even when a dog was a hopeless cripple, it was no easier to dispose of it than if it were a healthy specimen. In fact, it was sometimes more difficult.

Russ knew, and he thought on it now. But he thought also about how the hopelessly crippled dog in a kennel which housed thousands was really no dog at all, just a shadow creature hanging to the edge of life. And he remembered the law of the kennel. How could he forget it? It had been drummed into him, and he thought about it now, about how an animal, being no good to itself or to anyone, was better dead.

But was Gray to be put in that classification? Wasn't he still a vibrant animal pulsing with life?

And, if he had to die, wouldn't it be the coward's way to lead him to where a stranger's gun must do the job? Wasn't it his responsibility? If there was to be a killing, if Gray must be disposed of, wasn't it his job? Shouldn't he pull the trigger? If death was the sentence, shouldn't a friend get the call, so death might come as mercifully as such a thing can be?

Still, how could death ever be merciful when the victim was as strong, healthy, and full of life as the huge wolf? How could anyone call killing a healthy animal a humane act?

Russ knew there had to be some other way. Life wasn't created to be snuffed out on a whim — whether it be the life of a man, or, he thought, of this wolf.

The drone of an airplane disturbed his thoughts. He crawled to the edge of the forest to where he could look up. Coming straight at him was a slow-flying Piper Cub, dipping its wings first to one side and then the other as the pilot, and perhaps a passenger, obviously searched the forest for a sign of the wolf.

Russ scrambled back beneath the skirt of a spruce. Why an airplane? Was it being used to search for them? If it was, and if Gray was in the open, they could spot him instantly. He waited. The drone of the airplane faded. They hadn't seen the wolf, and now there was no sound except the low hum of a bumblebee tardily searching for nectar in a clump of purple asters on the edge of the marsh.

The boy got to his feet and moved deeper into the forest. Several hundred yards and he came to a scattering of feathers where Gray had obviously paused to eat the pheasant. The hungry wolf had gulped everything except legs and wing tips, and there were a few drops of blood already turned black on the pine needles.

Gray would probably head for the creek to drink, so Russ kept going. Where the pine gave way to a scattering of bare-boned alder bushes and some almost naked birch, he saw the glint of water. He slowed down, looking carefully from right to left for the wolf. When he didn't see the animal he continued downstream to where the banks were high enough to hold the water strictly to the channel, and then sat down to wait.

He heard the wolf before he saw him. Gray whined softly, and then Russ, tuning his eyes to the task of sorting out specific objects, spotted first the animal's eyes and then his ears. Gray was standing across the creek in a clump of white birch and tag alders and the intertwining branches formed a perfect camouflage.

"Taste good?" the boy asked, speaking loud enough so the wolf could hear him. Gray took a step forward so his huge head was fully visible. "You might at least have given me a drumstick."

Gray whined, almost as though he had understood the boy, and Russ tried to reassure the animal by saying, "I'm kidding. It's okay, Gray. It's okay."

4

GRAY WATCHED the boy carefully for a few seconds, and then, lowering his head, drank. When he finished he crossed the creek. It was then that the drone of another aircraft intruded.

Russ recognized it at once as the far-off roar of a helicopter. Now his amazement increased. Why would they go to the trouble and expense of putting up aircraft to catch one wolf?

Well, no matter, now they'd have to be well hidden to escape detection. Such a low-flying machine could hover and men using high-powered glasses could carefully scrutinize every foot of terrain.

They'd have to hide in new growth, among

young red pines so dense even a warbler would have trouble flitting through. There were many such stands of trees, especially in the kettlelike depressions which pocked the forest floor.

"Let's go!" he said sharply to the wolf, and getting up he took off at a lope. Gray, surprised by the sudden move, only stood watching until the boy disappeared among the trees. Then he lowered his tail and, guiding on the scent of the boy hanging in the air, loped after him.

Russ ran until his lungs felt like twin firebrands in his chest. Then he slowed to a walk and climbed a knoll which he knew looked down on a stand of ten-year-old trees which hadn't been thinned and stood greenly solid as a wall.

The roar of the helicopter was close when he topped out, so he ran again and then, at the edge of the planting, dropped to his knees and ducked under. At once he turned to watch for the wolf.

He saw the helicopter first, an ungainly prehistoric-looking birdlike creature hovering over the creek area they had just left. The machine made a circle of the creek area as though the men in it might have sighted something. Russ wondered if Gray had lingered.

The boy knew that once the helicopter spotted them it would follow wherever they went and direct the posses on the ground by radio. If the men in the aircraft sighted the wolf, the hunt would be over.

The helicopter was switching its bony tail from left to right as though the pilot couldn't make up his mind which course to fly. Then it pointed its grotesque, belly-heavy body in the boy's direction.

"You'd better come now," Russ said, as though the wolf were near enough to hear him. As if the words had triggered Gray into action, he came popping over the crest of the hill to scramble across the rocky glade and scoot beneath the canopy of pines.

Russ could hear Gray panting, and by pressing close to the ground, he could peer beneath the boughs and see a patch of white where the wolf lay.

For the moment they were safe. The helicopter came over, hovered for a few minutes above the trees, and then staggered on.

One thing now was obvious. Now that the hunt had taken to the air, they couldn't travel during the day. If they were to look for food, it would have to be at night. Daytime would have to be spent in the thickest cover they could find.

Russ got up and, parting the pines, walked toward the wolf. Gray was flat to the ground with his ears back. When he saw that he had come too close, he took a few steps back and then sank to his stomach on the ground.

Though he had just had a drink, he was thirsty again. His stomach, which had been hurting him, was numb. For the first time he felt a weakness in his legs and arms and a lightness in his head. He'd have to get food tonight or he'd be in bad shape by this time tomorrow.

The drumming of his heart slowed to a rhythmical thump as he relaxed, and a lethargy crept over him. So, why not sleep, he thought. There was nothing else he could do. He put his arms out and laid his head on them. The sandy soil beneath was warm. He looked over at the wolf. Gray had his eyes closed. His muzzle was on his forepaws. But Russ knew that should even a twig snap, or the breeze bring an unfriendly scent, the wolf would be instantly alert.

Sleep came easily. But once asleep, he had a torturous time dreaming that he was sitting at his own kitchen table unable to eat while his mother piled all manner of foods before him.

Then the dream faded and in his sleep he

heard a persistent belling coming as from far away and at regular intervals, like the tolling of some great and well-regulated church chime. It intruded on his sleep and persisted until it awakened him. Then he knew it was no dream, but the tolling of a hound methodically following a trail and at regular intervals bellowing about its progress.

Russ looked at once to the wolf. Gray had heard and recognized it for what it was. His head was up. His ears were forward to better catch the sound. The tip of his tongue showed red at the end of the muzzle. The white hairs of his body were bristling.

It was obvious the hound was being employed to run them out into the open so the helicopter might spot them so the ground gangs might close in.

Russet guessed the hound was nearly a mile away and would still have to untangle the skein of tracks where they'd made the pheasant kill, where they'd stopped at the side of the creek — but, from there on, the tracking would be easy and swift.

Well, he couldn't panic now. He looked up at the sun and was thankful it had started down the western side of the sky. If they could hold off until dark they could lay a trail in the forest that would drive even the best hound frantic.

"How do you like being hunted?" Russ asked the wolf, and he couldn't help but see the humor of it because, except for a very brief moment in most recent history, the wolf had been the hunter. Considering how long wolves had been on earth, it was only like yesterday that man came with his dogs to take the trail, precipitate the fight — kill the wolf.

The dog trailing them had come to where they'd killed the pheasant. Russ was sure of it, because of a hesitancy in the baying as the animal followed first one lead and then another, trying to piece together the evidence of what had happened.

No matter. If the dog was good he'd untangle it, though it took him ten or fifteen minutes. But then there'd be another tangle of trails at the creek where they'd stopped to drink.

Russ looked again at Gray. The wolf seemed more composed, as though he was beginning to resign himself to being the hunted instead of the hunter.

But the boy knew Gray would never accept the chase with, say, the equanimity of the fox. There was something in the wolf's innermost fiber, some instinctive fear that other mammals didn't have, and it made the animal so wary of man that some had even been known to run parallel to the highways for a hundred miles because of the man-scent, rather than risk crossing them.

What a laugh, Russ thought, that the fairy-book wolf should eat the grandmother! One whiff of that grandmother's front stoop and the wolf would have run straightaway until he couldn't run anymore. And, what nonsense, those stories of trappers being stalked, attacked, and killed by wolves. Why one Canadian newspaper had a standing reward for evidence of proof that a wolf had ever made an unprovoked attack on a man, and none had ever come forward to collect it.

The hound had the trail untangled, and the deep belling bay came at regular intervals, as the dog moved smoothly along the straight and easy path they'd made in going to the creek.

The helicopter came over again, but this time it did not hover. Likely men on the ground were keeping men in the machine posted on the hound's progress, and they were all waiting for the moment when the dog would make them break cover and run for it.

The hound had come to the creek and his measured baying turned to baffled barks. Russ could almost see the dog running in circles trying to unravel the scent line so it might trail away from where he and Gray had tarried.

Russ tried to relax, but it was hard now. He knew it wouldn't be long, and the dog would be on a line again. But he needed to preserve his strength for whatever emergency might threaten.

A barely audible growl came from Gray at the instant the hound straightened out the trail and the baying once again became a purposeful beat of sound.

There were no planes in the immediate vicinity, so Russ scrambled to the knoll to look down. Far below and to the south he got glimpses of the dog moving among the trees. Then, when the animal came to a clearing, he got a good look and identified it as a bloodhound. He didn't know of anyone in the vicinity who had bloodhounds trained to trail, so they must have gone to a lot of trouble to bring in the dog, perhaps from some other state. But why? For one wolf it seemed incredible!

He slid back down off the knoll and returned to where the wolf waited. Then he said to Gray: "Come on. We're going to lay a little trail."

At the sound of the boy's voice the wolf got to his feet and followed as Russ pushed his way through the nearly impenetrable stand of pine.

The area of trees didn't likely cover more than five acres, so the boy circled. He back-tracked often and each time he did he would strike out at right angles to the trail before starting another circle. He laid a spiral of scent all the way around the tract of trees and then, burrowing right to the center heart of the grove, lay down at the edge of a small fire-clearing. He was wet with sweat, though it was a brisk day. His hair was full of pine needles and some had fallen down inside his shirt to make his skin itch.

Gray had followed faithfully along and now lay waiting. The dog was coming up the knoll, and then, quite suddenly, the baying bore down on them with a loud blast of sound as the hound topped out.

Russ estimated there was still two hours of daylight left. It was too much. Even though they'd laid an intricate trail, the hound would unravel it before night.

Well, there was nothing else. It was as much as he could do.

The hound must have come full tilt down the hill because they could hear the rocks rolling. Then he knew the dog had come to where the scent was thick and hot for their having lain so long, because the hound forgot decorum and squeaked and squealed almost hysterically.

The triumph was brief, and the next tentative yips indicated bewilderment.

"Let him work on that awhile," Russ said, and the wolf put his tongue to his nose as though in acknowledgment.

For a while there was complete silence. Russ lifted to an elbow and strained forward hoping to hear better. The wolf lifted to his paws and peered out from beneath the overhanging boughs. But there was no sound from the dog.

A breeze began stirring the trees. It cooled the boy's face, blew a bead of moisture from the wolf's lolling tongue, and coughed softly through the long needles of the red pines. But it irritated Russ. The wind was covering sounds, keeping from him things he had to know.

He sat up and, opening his mouth wide and cupping both ears with his hands, he leaned forward to trap any sound the dog might make. Still, there was nothing.

"It isn't like a hound to quit," Russ said quietly to Gray. "Could be he got a thorn in a pad and is trying to dig it out with his teeth. Then again, this breeze . . ."

It hit Russet then. The wind was blowing directly from them to the hound. It would carry their odor and surely the hound would be turned from the trail to this fresher scent line, even though it was hung on such a tenuous thing as air.

"Gray, he's going to get us," the boy said, and at that instant the hound squealed sharply and then bayed with a staccato which indicated he was giving voice with every bounce he made.

Russet's inclination was to run, but he couldn't decide in which direction or where to run to. He could hear planes again. The men were surely not far behind the dog; and then, before he could decide on any course of action, the hound was in the clearing and he could see the long ears flopping, the heavy flews foaming, and the massive chest heaving as the animal bore down on them.

Russ didn't see Gray leave the cover of pines because the sight and sound of the hound had engulfed his senses. By the time he realized the wolf's intent, it was too late.

Without even a growl of warning Gray

had his jaws clamped across the hound's throat and was chomping through the loose folds of skin to get his teeth down to the warm blood of the throat.

It was a savagely primitive fight and Russ was overwhelmed by it. With a twist of his head and shoulders Gray had flipped the bloodhound on his back. Then Gray thrust and thrust and thrust again to get through the folds of tough hide which protected the huge neck.

It was like an assault on a rubber truck-tire, but now Gray was not to be denied, and a tooth went through and then he ripped until he had a hold and, in seconds, blood jetted to stain the wolf's white chest and Russ knew the dog was dead.

Gray disdained to give the carcass even a parting shake but slunk quickly out of the clearing for the protection of the pines.

Russ heard his own breath leave his body in a resounding groan. It had been as terrifying as a dream from which there was no escape, and for a while the boy was like one just awakened from some nightmare. Finally, he rubbed a hand across his face. Then he put his fingers to his eyes, and feeling the fingers, his sense of the reality of it all returned.

"Now we're really in for it," he whispered.

The wolf was standing trying to clean the blood from his chest with his long, pink tongue. The dog lay out there in the sun and already a few flies had found the body.

"Gray, we've got to get out of here," the boy said.

There was some assurance in the sound of his own voice, and getting to his feet he bulldozed his way through to the perimeter of pines. He stopped, looked to the sky for planes, and dashed across a clearing to a poplar grove. He followed among the milky trunks of poplar to what once had been a fence line and where wild grapes still grew. He ran the fence line up and over a hill and then dived into another grove of young pine and, crouched in concealment, watched until he saw the wolf come down the slope to hide beside him.

5

IN THEIR NEW HIDEOUT they lay still, listening for sounds of pursuit, but there was nothing except the hum of the planes and the wind in the trees. Russ would have blotted it all out with sleep, but when he closed his eyes he always saw the wolf take the hound by the throat and flip him over on his back as easily as he might have turned a bone over to get better leverage.

Finally just at sunset he dozed. When he awakened it was dark, and suddenly he was ravenously hungry. He sat up and looked for Gray. He saw him — indistinctly now — getting to his feet to stretch and open his jaws in a wide yawn.

"We have to find something to eat," Russ said. The wolf stretched again and he yawned again and the yawn ended with an anxious little whine.

"Don't complain," the boy said, "you had a whole pheasant today."

Russ knew he couldn't eat anymore of the tangy little wild apples. He had already eaten so many they were making him sick. That's all I need now, he thought, is a siege of green-apple dysentery.

But what else was there? He might find a fish or two in a creek backwater, but now he couldn't risk a fire to cook them, and he couldn't stomach them raw. Stripping vines of their dry berries at night would take forever. Frogs? Snakes? Even if he could find any, they'd still need a fire to render them edible.

"We have to raid someone's kitchen," Russ told the wolf.

The thought had been in the back of his mind most of every hungry moment, except that stealing was rupturing that part of the moral code which needed some thought. Then, obviously, there was the danger of discovery.

Strangely, it was no serious strain on his conscience to keep the countryside in an uproar by helping the wolf remain free. In his own rule book, the wolf had as much right to live as the people who were so righteously and wrathfully trying to run him to ground.

But stealing?

He had to think on that, because in the Clagg household theft ran a close second to such crimes as murder — even the theft of a dollar, and especially the theft of a dog.

Except, who would be hurt by the loss of one loaf of bread?

Well, he had to steal or he had to go home and call it quits. For himself he could end it that easily. Only for the wolf it wouldn't be over. They'd hunt him all the harder, rag him until they backed him starved right up against his own backbone. And then they'd shoot him.

So Russ got on with it. In his thoughts he again laid out the whole area around with its roads and lanes and creeks, its farmhouses and tree plantings, its pastures and marshes, and then he located himself on the map he had envisioned.

The closest house was the DuBarry's. The father worked in Milwaukee while his wife and daughters ran a riding stable. They had a large comfortable home. Their barns were painted and in repair. Their horses were fat.

They'd never miss such food as he and the wolf needed.

Once decided he didn't hesitate but got to his feet and, breaking out of the pines onto cleared ground, started toward a gravel road which he knew would take him to the DuBarry place. He walked the edge of the road, but did not come out onto it. Staying on the forest side of the hedgerow which lined the road, he paralleled it until he came to the open fields where the horses were pastured. Crawling into a clump of hazel brush he stretched out to reconnoiter.

The house was dark. A dim light burned in a hen house. In the field were shapes of horses — black and white and mottled. He knew he could walk through the animals without frightening them. All day they were ridden by strangers. The scent of someone they didn't recognize wouldn't spook them.

The DuBarrys must be gone. He looked at his watch. There was still ten minutes before nine o'clock. They couldn't be in bed. Well, maybe that was good — if they didn't come home while he was in the house.

He crawled from the hazel brush and, slipping beneath the lower strand of fencing, stood up. He looked and listened. There was only the sounds of horses — comfortable, satisfied sounds of weary horses breathing contentedly, grazing intermittently, blowing or shaking, and the sharp but tiny chink of small stones against iron shoes.

He looked back to the wolf. Gray had not moved, but was a white patch against the darker brush, obviously wary and reluctant now to move any closer to the buildings.

"Whoa, boy. Whoa." He talked quietly to the horses as he moved among them. Several followed along, hoping perhaps for a handout.

At the pasture gate he dropped to his knees to again look and listen. There was something by the barn. He crouched lower. It was a white duck. The house was silent so he opened the gate, slipped through and, closing it, hurried across the yard. He ducked into the back entry way, stopped again, and held his breath so it wouldn't interfere with his hearing.

Something brushed against his leg and, instinctively, he lunged forward and the kitchen door burst open when he hit it. Turning, he braced to meet whatever the hallway held. Then he heard a soft "meow" and it came to him that it was only a cat rubbing against his leg.

He found a chair and sat in it to compose

himself. Gradually the layout of the kitchen came into focus. There was the stove, a refrigerator, the sink. . . .

Getting up he went to the refrigerator and swung open the door. The inside light illuminated the kitchen. Half a large beef roast stood on a plate and he grabbed it. There were quart cartons of milk. He took a full one. Passing over the preserves and such edibles as would be difficult to carry, he closed the door. The kitchen went dark so he opened it again.

The bread box was on a counter next to the sink. He opened it and took out two loaves, grabbed a newspaper from a pile on a stool, and wrapped up the beef. Then he hurriedly closed the refrigerator door and carefully closing the kitchen door eased out into the yard.

A car was coming down the gravel road. He could hear stones kicking up against the fenders. With his arms full of bread, milk, and meat he had trouble with the gate. As he was about to close it the lights turned into the DuBarry drive.

Russ ran. Frightened, the horses knotted together, and when he raced toward them they exploded in every direction and then grouped again to go thundering toward the gate. There was room for one horse to get through at a time, but the whole herd hit the gate and Russ heard it splinter.

He ran so fast he forgot about the pasture fence; and wire caught him across the throat and he was slammed backward. He lay for a moment trying to recover his breath and his senses, and then, without getting up, he crawled the rest of the way and rolled into the hazel brush.

Looking back he could see the horses galloping in and out of the beams from the car headlights.

People were shouting. A yard light came on. Some of the horses were galloping down the drive to the road. Ducks quacked. Chickens in the hen house cackled. A dog which likely had been in the car began to bark.

Russ rolled deeper into the brush. Then when he was far enough to get up without being seen, he jumped to his feet and ran. He sensed Gray was near, though he couldn't see the wolf. No matter. The wolf would find him. Now all he wanted was to put distance between himself and the farm before the DuBarrys discovered someone had been in their house.

He followed on the hedgerow until he heard hoof beats. Some of the horses must have headed down the road in the same direction he was running. He veered abruptly and once in the brush slowed to a walk.

The creek would be as good a place as any to spend the night. It would be easy to come to. All he had to do was get into a coulee and follow it to the bottom. Here, all coulees ran like fingers down to the creek, and in spring they carried run-off water to feed it.

Gray still hadn't shown himself when he started down the long, slow slant of terrain which would bring him to the bottoms. He hoped the wolf hadn't panicked. It wasn't likely. He'd find him. He could follow a trail as well or better than any hound.

The temptation to sit right down and eat was great, but he wanted to put more distance between himself and the farm before he did. A half-moon had risen and he could see the creek winding like a silver thread below.

Now he would wait, if only for a little while, to see that he didn't get too far out front of Gray. The instant he stopped he saw the wolf to his left and realized that Gray had been staying within smelling distance, but just out of sight, probably all the way.

"Okay, Gray, I see you," he said softly. The wolf stopped and turned toward him.

"Just getting something to eat," he explained, as though the animal knew what he was talking about.

He went right to the edge of the water before dropping to his knees and putting down the food. He cupped his hands and rubbed his face with the cool water, and then bent over to drink. Gray came to the bank and lay a short distance downstream watching.

Now he couldn't wait. Tearing the waxed wrappers off the bread, he threw the wolf a loaf, and began tearing chunks from the other loaf and cramming them into his mouth. At the taste of food his mouth filled with saliva and ran down his chin. He swallowed hard several times and felt the bread hit his stomach as though made of stone. He stopped eating and was bent double by the pain. He dropped the loaf and, getting to his hands and knees, vomited.

Sitting back he looked over to the wolf. He knew he had made a spectacle of himself, but Gray's attention was focused on the loaf which he held between his forepaws and he was eating deliberately, instead of with what some have mistakenly called wolfish eagerness.

The pain left and he couldn't hold back a laugh. Get something to eat and almost choke eating it, he thought. Well, he'd take it easy. He opened the milk carton and took a few sips. It was sweet and cool and as delicious as anything he could ever remember having passed his lips. He sipped again and then tore off a small piece of bread and, after chewing slowly, swallowed it. He followed the bread with a sliver of meat. Then he drank more milk.

When his first hunger had been assuaged, he broke the bone out of the roast and threw it to the wolf.

Gray sniffed the meat cautiously and then tried it with his tongue.

"It's good," Russ assured the animal. "Try it."

Russ wrapped what was left of the food in the newspaper. He could have eaten more, but instead satisfied himself with the rest of the milk.

Gray had cleaned the meat from the bone and now, with a single bite, he broke the bone into two nearly equal parts and then, without any further chewing, swallowed each half.

"No wonder people are scared of you," he told the wolf. "If you have to eat like that, never do it in public."

He lay back comfortably suffused with the

warmth a full stomach can give. There were problems to ponder and decisions to be made, but right now he was going to enjoy this after-dinner lethargy.

"Man, Gray," he said, speaking softly so as not to break the mood the night had put over him, "it would be great to live out like this if the weather stayed nice and a guy had plenty to eat."

The moon seemed to be sailing swiftly, there were so many wispy clouds being blown across the face of it. He was watching it through the bare branches of a tall, white birch where a single leaf still twirled on a broken stem.

Lying there, it seemed to him, the leaf was wild to get away. In the wind it tugged at the stem which tethered it, struggling to be released. Then, even while he watched, the tree relinquished its hold on the last leaf and it sailed away, twisting and turning as though hysterically grateful it had at last been freed.

Russ sighed deeply and so did the wolf, and it was hard to believe that they were being hunted — that they were not able to move freely from valley to hill, forest to forest, river to river, with the wind whichever way it blew.

But Russ knew soon there would be snow

and, with winter on them, they'd come by really hard times.

Enjoy it while you can, the boy thought, and he locked his hands behind his head, sighed again, and lay back. As though on cue the wolf lay down, and there was only the small creek making small gurgling sounds around a log, over a boulder, up against the bank of a sharp bend.

Perhaps they might have spent the night there on the creek bank beneath the birch trees, except that, just as a dark cloud passed over the moon, a weird and wild howl came thinly on the wind.

Gray leaped to his feet as though stung by a bullet. Russ sat bolt upright. He felt the little hairs on his neck rise and every hair along his arms lift, and he knew, even before the last tremolo was lost and gone among the other sounds of the night, that he had heard another wolf calling.

"Impossible!" Russ said it so loudly and sharply that Gray turned his head and bristled at the harsh intrusion of a human voice.

Hardly believing, Russ stood up and bent far forward as though straining to catch an echo or some clue to the origin of that wild wail. But now there was nothing, except that when he looked over at Gray, he saw the wolf was veritably tingling with excitement.

Perhaps it had been a dog, and both he and Gray were mistaken. People claimed that dogs, anticipating a death, could howl with almost the exact same tremolo as a wolf. Russ didn't believe it. He had heard many a dog howl, but it was never with the same passionate and lonely wildness which characterized Gray's quavering call on such nights as he had sat by the kennel door with sharp nose thrust toward the high, full moon.

Or maybe it had only been the wind trapped by some strange angle in the bole of an old and rotting tree. The wind could make strange noises: soft and sighing through the long needles of a red pine, sharper and more brisk through the shorter needles of a white pine. Bone rattling in the leaves of an oak reluctant to look like death. It could make piercing sounds through vines. The wind had many voices.

But a wolf? Why, there weren't, there couldn't be any in the Kettle Moraine!

Russ felt his muscles which had come taut gradually grow limp again. He looked over at the wolf. Gray was on his haunches trying the air with his nose.

"Maybe even a siren," Russ said. The new sirens made weird noises. "Maybe even a siren," he repeated. But hardly had he said it when he heard the howl, and this time there was no doubt in the boy's mind that he was listening to the wailing of a wolf.

That it was incredible made it no less real. It was as real and true as the moon and the trees around him. It was a wolf howling, surely as he was a boy and he was in the forest with Gray and they were being hunted.

He got to his feet and marveled at how long the wolf could sustain the howl without needing to breathe. Now he no longer wondered *how* it could be a wolf, but only *what* wolf could it be, and from *where* was the howl coming?

A half-mile at the very most, he thought, because the sound was coming against the wind. Probably at New Lake clearing, where the Conservation Department had gouged out a large pond and was in the process of clearing land so campers might have a place to fish and swim.

"What do you think?" Russ asked, turning. But Gray had gone, and though the boy involuntarily shouted: "Come back!" it was obvious nothing could stop the animal.

Russ started after him.

6

THE MOON HELPED light the boy's way through the thickets. It was bright enough so that he distinctly saw the ripe, purple-red fruit of a wild plum and made a mental note of its location in the event there'd be time for dessert on this night of the strange wolf's howling.

At first he tried to overtake Gray, but the wolf was traveling too swiftly. So, he settled for a cross-country lope, slowing only where brambles scratched at him, where prickly ash tore at his trousers, and where ivy and grape and wild cucumber vines put up such a wall he had to break his way through.

He hadn't gone a half-mile when the wolf howled again. He stopped to listen. The howl began thinly and then became a full-throated resonance that went on and on to a quavering conclusion.

He had often listened in amazement when Gray had howled. The undulations of sound, all in the same key, were a marvel of musical control. The wolf accomplished it by compressing and then loosening his lips after the manner of an opera singer, and he had never seen any dog quite able to duplicate the wolf's facility at so shivering a sound.

Listening to the wail he felt a wave of weakness pass. He had heard that for a man left alone in a forest the wolf's howl could be an almost mesmerizing experience.

Well, he couldn't afford to be hypnotized, not by the howling of a strange wolf. He shook himself almost with the dexterity of a dog and was about to start forward when another howl came up from the bottomland through the trees, through the brakes, across the marshes.

It was Gray. He was answering the call, and if there was a difference between the howling of the strange one and his wolf, it was difficult to detect.

Judging from the location of the howl,

Gray must be closing in on the strange wolf. Russ didn't wait for the howl to narrow to a thin trembling, but started down the gentle slope at a run.

He still couldn't believe there was another wolf loose in the Kettle Moraine Forest but, if there was, he wanted to see for himself, and he wanted to see what happened when Gray and the strange one met.

He went through the thickets with such abandon his clothes were being shredded. There was blood on his forehead and one cheek, but he never knew it. A pants leg was torn from ankle to knee, but he didn't notice the flapping cloth. He was determined to be in on the rendezvous, because it might prove to be the climactic end to his long nights and hungry days of running — the end of the boy-wolf pact — Gray's final bid for freedom.

The pond came in view quite abruptly. It lay like a silver dollar beneath the moon. Huddled close to the water were outhouses and a large shelter where campers might cook when rain put out their tent-side fires. At the edge of the clearing where the white sand began, Russ dropped to his knees and put his bundle of food on the ground beside him.

Nothing moved in the clearing which was several hundred yards across. Sometimes a gust of wind got far enough below the border of conifer trees to scuff the water and break the silver shine of the pond, but other than that, he might have been looking at a painting which the artist had satin-shined with moonbeams.

Perhaps he had misjudged and the wolf cry was not, after all, emanating from this place but from somewhere beyond. Surely, if there was a wolf out there, he would see it. The area had been cleared of every stick of brush, and the only hiding places were the outhouses and the shelter.

Knowing wolves, Russ was sure none would seek refuge beneath a roof. They'd make a wide circle to avoid even remote contact with civilization. He was on the verge of getting up and walking out into the clearing, hoping by showing himself to bring Gray into the clearing too. He felt sure the wolf was somewhere nearby, even crouching perhaps, as he was, on the edge of the cover looking out across the sand.

He got to one knee and then dropped back to the ground, when from right out in front of him, a wolf began howling. For a second he couldn't believe that he was hearing a wolf. The howl came from the clearing but there was nothing there! Nothing. Only footprints, like shadows on the sand, footprints of many men and nothing more.

It was like standing in a bare and empty room listening to a voice. It was like standing in the middle of a wilderness and suddenly hearing music. It was inexplicable!

For a second time Russ shook himself vigorously to get a grasp on reality. He heard the wolf. It was howling right out there in front of him, but he couldn't see it.

Then it hit him — the whole terrible truth of the trap! He was so stunned by the audacity and cunning he was unable to decide on a course of action, and then Gray broke precipitously from cover. He loped across the white sand, bright in the moonlight, a huge wolf, with tongue lolling in anticipation, heading for death.

A cry of warning was locked in the boy's throat. It was held there by the rattle of gunfire. Russ could see tiny spurts of flame coming from the buildings. Then, strong searchlights cut across the sand, across the water to pinpoint the wolf. He saw Gray trying to elude the lights the way a frantic fly tries to elude the little gray flycatcher.

He heard the smack of a bullet. It was the

thud a hunter learns to recognize as a hit into flesh. He saw Gray go down and saw sand fly upward into the beam of a light. The shooting stopped. Men began pouring from the buildings and Russ watched, no longer horrified, only coldly sick, deep down inside.

The men sounded jubilant, as though they'd won a war, and Gray lay there only a little whiter than the sand. Russ felt like vomiting again. He looked away, hoping the sick feeling would leave. It was while his eyes were averted that the sudden change from victory to chagrin sounded in the men's voices. He turned his head quickly.

Gray was up and running. Sand flew. Guns sounded. Lights came back on. Then, the white wolf vanished in the brush and, for a moment, there was such silence as can only come over a group as when it is completely stunned by the turn of events.

But the posse was not silent for long. Some cursed. Others urged pursuit. And all converged on the spot where the wolf had gone down.

"He's hard hit," Russ heard one of the men say, "just look at all the blood." And with the moon on the sand Russ had seen the blood, a black stain.

Emotionally the boy felt as though he'd

been wrung out and hung up to dry. He didn't even hate the men. He only wanted to leave that place, get away. Slowly he backed off until he was safely from sight. Then he got to his feet and, clutching the bundle of food under his arm, began to walk.

He walked as though in a daze, brushing up against trees and even falling. When he was back at the creek he lay down beside it.

After a while he felt better. Crawling, he lay over the bank and dunked his head under water.

The icy creek pressed against his hot eyelids, against his throbbing temples. He held his breath, kept his head down, and then when he couldn't hold his breath any longer, he came up blowing water. Twice he submerged his head and held his breath. Then he wiped his face on his shirt sleeve.

The moon was almost directly above. He decided to put some distance between himself and the place where they'd shot Gray. But he walked carefully now, avoiding bramble patches, skirting the dense growths of young pine, going around the bottom of knolls, walking the rims of the kettles — and by midnight he had come to the cliff where the posse had almost trapped him and the wolf.

It might be the last place they'd look, he

thought. And, if there was a chance Gray was still alive, he might track him to this place.

Russ went up the cliff the back way, the route he'd taken when they'd made their run for it. He dropped over the little wall to the shelf and to the cave entrance. He sat on the shelf and tried to eat but couldn't. Then, he crawled into the cave and, pushing together leaves and grass he had gathered on their last visit, made a nest and was soon asleep in it.

It was a frantic night there alone with his dreams in the little cave. Once, in a wild swinging nightmare, he hit the stony sides of his shelter so hard he cut his hands. Sometimes, when a dream would awaken him, he'd crawl to the cave mouth and sit staring out into the night hoping to see the wolf's eyes watching him. But there was nothing.

The sun came up even before the moon had dropped out of the sky, and when Russ came from the cave there was a big, bright orb on the eastern horizon and a misshapen, pale stone of moon slipping away in the West.

He sat for a long time looking out over the low green cover of the Big Burn to where the sumac still showed enough red to identify a fire break, to where some elms towered above surrounding pines to mark a forester's trail, to the far, far away hill that was home.

He scanned the edges of all the clearings carefully, hoping for a glimpse of Gray, but not quite believing he would get one. He gave a low whistle, the one he used to alert the wolf to his presence. But, if Gray were in the vicinity, he chose not to show himself, and this might be entirely possible because Russ knew that the seriously wounded of the animal world prefer to suffer in solitude.

Even dogs, on being grievously injured, will crawl away to die alone. And cats, sensing the approach of death, will likely wander off to meet the end on their own terms.

Well, there was no question in his mind. He would have to wait. To go home now was out of the question. He would have to stay at least until he was reasonably sure the wolf was dead, and he felt that in some way, somehow, Gray would permit it — let him know.

Anyway, this morning there was food. He crawled into the cave and came back out into the sunshine with the meat and bread. Unwrapping it, he made a sandwich. It would be dry without water, but it would be good. He was bringing the sandwich to his mouth when a headline in the paper in which the food had been wrapped caught his attention.

The food never got to his lips, but stopped halfway there while he read:

TRAP TIGHTENS AROUND KILLER WOLF

HUNTERS TO EMPLOY RECORDED HOWLS OF WILD WOLVES TO ENTICE KETTLE MORAINE MAVERICK WITHIN RANGE OF HUNTERS' GUNS

Russ had known the wolf howls had been recorded, but not until after the shooting had started. He was surprised that he hadn't thought of it before. The trouble had been that he just couldn't believe there was a reason for such an all-out effort to get Gray when all he had done was kill a dog.

The boy put the sandwich down and smoothed out the grease-stained paper. Turning so the sunlight came over his shoulder to illuminate the smaller lettering which had been smudged, he read:

By Staff Correspondent

Eagle, Wis. — A recording made in the wilds of Canada of wolves howling was to be played tonight on high-fidelity equipment in an effort to tempt from hiding the wolf believed to have killed Russet Clagg, 15-year-old son of Mr. and Mrs. Cal Clagg of Woodbine Drive in the Kettle Moraine Forest.

Incredible! Russ couldn't believe it. They thought he was dead!

Young Clagg disappeared four days ago when he followed the wolf into the forest after the animal broke its leash and killed a prize boxer dog. No one has seen boy or wolf since, though a trap was robbed of its bait, a farmer's lamb was killed by the wolf, and wolf tracks have been seen at various places in the forest.

But then, why hadn't they seen his tracks? But perhaps not. There were lots of human tracks in the forest, but only one wolf was leaving paw prints. Then, too, search parties sometimes defeated themselves by trampling any evidence which might have been read and interpreted by more expert trackers.

If the wolf recording fails to lure the wolf to gun, Bernard (Bull) Shott, self-appointed coordinator of the hunt and president of Head Hunters, Inc., a local big-game shooting club, has said: "We'll spread poison!"

Wisconsin Conservation Department officials warned Shott and other hunters that timber wolves are protected in the state, and that laying of poison is not only contrary to state but many local laws.

Sade Svenson, county warden, has repeatedly urged citizens to stay out of the Kettle Moraine area because they are hampering efforts to locate the wolf.

Shott belittled efforts of the state. "As usual," he said, "they are too late and they are coming with too little."

Hunters have converged from all over the southern part of the state to get in on the hunt. Svenson said the gangs were becoming a danger one to the other.

Meanwhile, intrigued by hunt for the white wolf, representatives of newspapers, radio, and television stations from all over the country continue to arrive at Milwaukee's General Mitchell Field. The story of the wolf hunt has pushed war, riot, and political news to the inside pages of the paper.

Russ had to stop to assimilate what he had read. Sitting there alone on the ledge with the quiet and seemingly peaceful countryside spread out before him it was difficult to believe that his disappearance had triggered such a hysterical reaction.

As it dawned on him that people everywhere were talking about him and the wolf, and that millions of people were awaiting word of Gray's death and the discovery of his body, he went cold and felt goose pimples prickle his arms.

He had realized from his voluminous reading that wolves were capable of striking terror into the hearts of the ignorant, those who remembered old engravings of wolf packs running down Russian sleds or entering the streets of ancient cities. . . .

But he had also come to believe that, in this supposedly enlightened country, the majority of people discounted all such wolf stories because by now there were enough agencies and publications disseminating the truth about the animals. But, obviously, it hadn't been enough. Or was all the hue and cry directly traceable to a blood-thirsty minority which reveled in the sadistic savagery of being part of an armed posse?

He didn't know, and probably neither did anyone else. It seems there had been a spark and then a small blaze and then a wind had come up, and the whole forest was on fire. That was about the way it must have happened. Like the riots he'd read about starting from a single, trivial incident and spreading through a city in concentric circles until everyone was involved.

He shook his head still not believing. Then, with the torn sleeve of his shirt, he wiped a smear of grease from the paper and continued to read:

> Cal Clagg, the boy's father, still does not believe his son is dead. "I don't believe the wolf would kill him," Clagg said. "They were very close, and I even think the wolf thought Russ was just another wolf, a younger animal he was supposed to care for."

Well, anyway, his family had maintained their sanity. It was like them though, but now surely he'd have to get word to them that he really *was* well, that there was nothing to worry about.

He held the paper to the sun again to read through the tallow smears:

> Mrs. Clagg agrees with her husband. She claims if search parties would only

withdraw from the forest the boy and wolf would come home.

But the wishes of the Claggs aren't likely to be honored. Southeastern Wisconsin has been turned into an armed camp with helicopters flying reconnaissance.

Four dogs, all German shepherds, have already been mistakenly shot for wolves.

(*Continued on Page Four, Column One*)

Russ turned, but there was no page four. The inside pages of the paper were missing. He folded the paper back together and, putting his sandwich and the rest of the meat and bread on it, wrapped the food. He couldn't eat. He had to think.

7

BY NOON Russ had come to terms with himself, had made some decisions. He felt better now that he had a plan of action, and he was able to eat the sandwich.

There had been no sign of the wolf, but three times during the morning search parties had come within view, and one had passed so close he could hear the voices of the men as they barged through the kettles and the cover.

If it hadn't all been so tragic Russ might have laughed at them. What wolf would blunder blindly into such mobs as were crisscrossing the forest? But then, and the thought struck him in the pit of his stomach, perhaps instead of the wolf they were looking for his body.

It gave him an eerie feeling to sit there and think people were looking for his remains; yet, there was a fascination to his predicament — or, was it *their* predicament?

Here he sat warm in the sun with good bread and meat in his belly, as much alive as he'd ever been, and down there people were looking in the brush for his corpse. Perhaps this was the way it was when you really died and went up to some ethereal place from which you could look down and laugh or feel sorry for the people mulling about like ants on the great ant heap which was the earth.

Perhaps he should have slept since he had a busy night planned for himself; but with every nerve ending tingling to the possibility that Gray might try to come to him, he couldn't keep his eyes closed.

His common sense told him the wolf wouldn't show. Even if Gray were alive, he would hide out the daytime hours in the thickest cover. It wasn't likely, unless a search party spooked him, that he'd try to make contact before dark.

Planes came over intermittently during the afternoon, but then the day was almost over and the sunset was a magnificent skyful of brilliance as viewed from his high place. On the cliff, it seemed he could see right over the edge of the earth to where the colors were being mixed. Red was the mother color of them all, but when rays carried shafts of red into the sky they were diluted pink and salmon and sometimes they turned purple where clouds clustered.

Darkness came gently, lifting first in the valley below so he could watch the shadows creeping up toward him — across the tops of the pines, up from the still vivid green burn. He could see it edge closer up the cliff like an approaching shadow, until at last the night was around him. But still he waited, and then there came the moon — orange and larger this night — and he let it lift high enough to bleed white before striking out.

He went directly to the road which led to Woodbine Drive and, staying in the shadow of the hedgerow, headed west. It was cold. He shivered. This night there surely would be frost.

As he moved, he was constantly alert to the possible presence of Gray. He knew the wolf's habit of staying just out of sight, surmising, perhaps, that the boy could smell him so there was no need to visibly present himself.

There were some search parties abroad, but they didn't worry him. Twice, small groups came down the road and the men were laughing and talking as though on a holiday outing. He easily avoided them by going off into the brush and waiting until they passed.

When he came to Woodbine Drive he left the roadway and went cross-lots on a trail he'd traveled hundreds of times. It brought him to the rear of the kennels, and when the dogs smelled him they started to bark.

"Quiet!" he cautioned sharply, and they remembered and stopped barking.

Staying in the shadows he crossed the road and came through an oak grove to where he had a good view of the house. Lights were on in every room. There were cars in the drive. He heard a door open and close, heard voices, saw people cross the yard.

He crawled closer. There was a man with a camera. Another wore the uniform of the state police. He thought he saw his mother's silhouette through a lighted window. He heard his father's voice: "There's nothing more to say. We're tired. We'd like to go to bed. We'd like to . . ." Then the door closed and he couldn't hear him.

Well, he'd have to wait; so he slithered

back to where the oaks were thicker and, putting the small of his back against the trunk of a venerable tree, he tried to relax.

Cars began leaving the yard. Some turned east and others went west on Woodbine Drive. Lights went out in some rooms of the house. All of the yard lights except the one over the back porch were extinguished. He humped himself forward and getting to his hands and knees crawled closer. He was about to stand up when he felt a presence other than his own.

He dropped to his belly. Perhaps it had been a twig snapping. Maybe out of the corner of his eye he had seen a leaf move. Could be a hint of some strange odor had come to his nostrils. But maybe, as some claimed, he actually could *feel* — through his skin, his nerve ends, the hairs of his neck — that some other living thing had come to the oak grove and was eyeing him.

Slowly he turned his head. First left. Then right. Then he got to his hands and knees so he could look behind. Then he saw him. Barely visible. Indistinct as an apparition in the moonlight. Like mist. Gray, his great white wolf, back where the prickly ash was thick.

So Gray had come to this place instead of the cave on the cliff. It made sense. This really was the home place.

He wondered how long the wolf had been waiting. Maybe he'd been watching all the time. He didn't think so. The feeling of another's presence had been quite abrupt.

He wondered too why he didn't feel more thankful, more grateful that Gray was alive, and he supposed that down deep, down where it really counted, he hadn't believed the wolf was really dead.

"You're a regular darn spook," the boy said quietly as he crawled closer to the animal.

Gray whined softly, and Russ maneuvered close enough so he could look the wolf over in the moonlight. He was a ragtag wolf. His hair was dry and lifeless. His ruff was ragged and black in places with dried blood. The usually glistening nose was dry and cracked and pitted — possibly from fever. Without being able to clearly see them, Russ knew the eyes would be dull. The plume of a tail had burdocks matted in it. There were rashes of bootjack sticktights along both sides.

Russ tried to move closer to the wolf, but Gray got up and backed off.

"Still not ready?" Russ asked.

With the wolf standing the boy could see the wound. There was a long gash in his chest. The bullet had obviously knocked the wind out of the animal and that is why he had gone down. Some of the rifles were powerful enough to slam a man to the ground even if the bullet only hit him in the hand.

"Looks like you'll live," Russ said, and now for the first time, he felt a wave of emotion start deep inside and well upward bringing tears with it. He brushed at his eyes, and, coming to a sitting position, said: "Well, we're about back where we started."

There might have been a quick and decisive ending to the almost macabre event, Russ thought, if only the wolf would consent to being caught or to come in. He knew his father would stand beside them, even though Gray had killed a lamb and two dogs. But perhaps not. Maybe it was too late.

Anyway Gray seemed adamant. He was not going to give himself up. From deep down inside, perhaps from a primitive heritage over which he had no control, there must have been a yearning, a longing to run free as wolves had from the beginning of time. Perhaps even such a perilous freedom as he now enjoyed was better than submitting again to kennel or leash. Perhaps now death was preferable to imprisonment.

"I don't suppose I should blame you," Russ said. "Maybe I'd feel the same way."

He turned away from the wolf. There were

things to do. He crawled back to the edge of the oak grove to survey the house. There were no strange cars in the yard and only one light in the kitchen. He looked back. Gray had not moved. Getting up, Russ stepped into the yard clearing. He stood for a while as though waiting for something to happen. When nothing did, he went around to the kitchen and knocked gently on the door.

His mother opened it and then he was in her arms and she was crying. His father came over and hugged him too.

"They killed Gray?" his father made it a question.

Once again Russ had to rub his eyes because there were tears in them. For a moment he couldn't speak, then he said: "Only wounded. Pretty bad, but I'm sure he'll live."

"He won't come in?" Again his father made it a question.

"That's right. He won't come in."

"Will he stay with you?"

"Yes," the boy said, and now he could see how tired and worried they looked. His father — his hair looked grayer tonight — put his hand on his mother's shoulder. She was smaller by a foot than her husband and her hair was still raven black.

She moved forward to put a hand to Russ's cheek. "You look so thin. When did you last eat?"

"Today. I've had food."

"From DuBarrys'?" the father asked.

So they had heard. "Yes," and Russ couldn't help grinning as the thought of the horses clattering out of the pasture.

"What are you going to do?" the father asked, and it was just like him. He might well have said: "Now look here, Son, this is what you're going to do!" But no. He simply asked: "What are *you* going to do?"

Russ hesitated. This had always been the way with the Claggs. His parents would help if he asked them to. But if his plans ran contrary to theirs, they would permit him to at least *try* to solve the problem his own way.

"Well," he finally said, "if I stay here, abandon Gray, you know they'll have him within days. I know he's only a wolf, and I know a lot of people are concerned, but . . ." He hesitated again, as though the immensity of the public's reaction had first dawned on him.

"But perhaps you should. Maybe you must make yourself stay. What else can you do?" His mother said it softly, almost shyly, as though she knew she shouldn't try to influence the boy with such overconcern as a mother's love can generate.

Russ looked to his father for help. Cal Clagg only shrugged, but then thinking the boy might take it as a sign of indifference, said: "We can't help but feel concerned about your safety. Does the wolf matter that much?"

The boy hung his head and chewed thoughtfully on his lower lip. "It's more than the life of one wolf," he tried to explain. "It's something that's got to do with me. If I give up now — if I let them get Gray . . . I don't know. It will be as bad as though Gray were not a wolf at all, but some person, some friend whom I've turned in."

He lifted his head, looked to his parents, and his face plainly asked: "Do you . . . can you understand?"

There was silence in the kitchen then. But Mrs. Clagg's face seemed to relax, and the tight lines around her mouth smoothed away. The father came over to put a hand on the boy.

"But how?" he asked. "How can you save him?"

"By taking him north. Getting him into a

pack. There's supposed to be one in the Nicolet Forest. Maybe I can find it. Maybe they'll accept him."

"It will be a hard thing to do," the father said.

"I know."

"I don't see how," the mother said, and the tight little lines were again forming around her mouth.

"I could travel nights. It isn't that far. If I was lucky . . ."

Lights of a car flashed in the yard, through a window. Russ ducked as though someone had swung a fist trying to hit him.

"I've got to get out of here!"

"But you can't go like that," his mother almost wailed. "Look at yourself! Your clothes are ruined! You're cut! You're hurt!"

Russ headed for the side door. Over his shoulder he looked back to say: "Clothes. Food. Matches. You know," he said, opening the door to go out. "And a map. Yes, I'll need a map."

His father stepped through the door with him and closed the door gently behind. Now they whispered.

"I don't know what to say, Russ," the father said. "It's something which shouldn't be decided so quickly. You and the wolf, and your mother and I aren't the only ones involved. There's lots of people worrying, wondering. Is it right for us to let them continue thinking you are dead?"

The boy had no ready answer. Somewhere, out among the pines, a great horned owl gave fair warning to all the rabbits that he was coming hunting. Across the road, the dogs in the kennel heard and answered with a roar of many canine voices. Finally, with his mouth close to his father's ear, he said: "If you want me to stay, I will. If you say I can go, I'll head north. I'll do as you say."

Again there was a silence which seemed interminable. Only sound came from the house, and sometimes it didn't seem like sound at all because the voices coming through the door were muffled as the wind where there are too many pines for it to find its voice.

Finally the father said: "Go. We'll get clothes, fix a pack." He pushed the boy gently from him and, opening the door, went in. Warmth from the house rushed out. Then the door closed.

Russ stood quietly beside the house listening. Then, crouching, he hurried across the clearing and disappeared among the trees.

Gray was where he'd left him. Russ stayed

what the wolf would consider a respectable distance and sat watching the house. Two more cars arrived. Lights began to go on in the rooms again.

"They're sure having a time of it," Russ said, referring to his parents.

Anyway, now for sure, they knew he was alive, although it seemed they had never once believed that he was dead. Maybe most of the others didn't believe it either, Russ thought. Maybe most of the others had to have him dead or what excuse would they have to go on making such a big thing out of the wolf hunt?

It was like the time he'd helped kill a cat. The other boys, most of them older, had invented a whole lurid life for the Old Gray Cat. Murderer of birds! And they found some feathers to prove it. Cannibal! They said Old Gray Cat would eat her own kittens. Evil instrument of the devil, they said, because if Old Gray Cat should ever lie across the neck of any sleeping person, that one would go instantly insane.

He remembered how they'd talked it up until he'd come to hate Old Gray Cat, though in the heart of him he'd known she was innocent. Then, armed with self-righteousness, someone had gotten a gun and they'd sallied forth, and though he wasn't the one to pull the trigger, he now knew he was as guilty as the others because he had acquiesced.

He wondered if that was how it was with the hunters who'd come to kill Gray.

Cars were leaving again, and when they were all gone the light came on in his bedroom. He crawled to the edge of the trees and would have gotten up to walk over but another car arrived.

He decided not to risk going to the house. Someone might see him. Then surely they would force him into being an unwilling accessory to the fact of Gray's murder. Even his father wouldn't be able to prevent the killing. Not with the wolf running wild. The Kettle Moraine, with all its hikers and picnickers, was no place for a wolf — harmless or not. No one would permit it. They'd hunt until they killed or caught him, and Russ was certain now they'd never take Gray alive.

He went back to the hedge of prickly ash and resumed his place near the wolf. The light went out in his bedroom and then one came on in the basement. He could hear the telephone. A vapor haze lifted from the chimney so he knew the oil furnace had kicked in.

Around him the earth had begun to whiten with frost. This would be the coldest of all nights since he'd walked off into the woods to catch the wolf. It seemed so long ago that sometimes he felt it had all happened to someone else and he had only heard the story somewhere.

But the tremors which began to shiver him were painful evidence that he was the one it was happening to.

"At least you carry your winter underwear with you," he said to the wolf.

Russet's watch had stopped. He'd have to remember to keep it wound — but it must have been after midnight before the yard was completely deserted for the first time since he'd been inside.

He moved to the edge of the trees, but instead of leaving the shadows, he sat with his back to a tree to wait. He didn't have to wait long before the side door opened and he saw his mother and father come out.

"Over here," he said softly.

They came over. His mother handed him a bundle. "Warm clothes," she said.

His father handed him a packboard with pack attached. "Food, shelter-half, matches — you know, the works. I thought about a gun. Would you want one? It might only mean trouble."

"No. No gun," Russ said. He had half expected they might change their position, try to keep him home, but all they asked was where the wolf was.

"Back there," Russ pointed. They both stopped to look beneath the branches so they could see the patch of white back against the brush.

"Don't take any chances if they start shooting," his father warned.

"I won't."

He put the bundle of clothes under one arm and held the pack by the straps with his other hand.

"You didn't forget the map?" he asked.

"It's in there," his father said.

"Thanks."

"Just take care of yourself," the mother said.

"I will, Mother. I will." He put his face to her cheek and kissed her.

"If we could get him into the station wagon? We could take him north," his father said.

"He won't," Russ assured his father. "He won't let me get near enough to even get a rope on him."

Two cars were coming down the road. Both had spotlights and they were prying the brush with them. "I'd better go," the boy said. He started away.

"Good luck," the father said.

"God bless you and keep you." There was a sob in his mother's voice.

He took a few steps into the darker shadows under the oaks.

"If you need us call. Collect. Anytime. We'll come."

Russ turned and went back through the trees to the prickly ash hedge where the wolf waited.

8

THEY TRAVELED that night because Bull Shott's threat to poison Gray made the boy fearful of every inch of Kettle Moraine terrain. It was a danger against which he had no defense. The wolf's keen power of scent might bring him to a bait small even as a golf ball and then, before he, Russ, knew that it was there, Gray would have gulped it to die in such terrible paroxysms as a dose of strychnine can induce.

But first they stopped just short of Highway 67 which ran north and south through the forest, and Russ opened the bundle of clothes. Shivering violently, he got out of the tattered things he was wearing and into the warm clothes his mother had provided.

There was a suit of long underwear, and it clutched his legs and arms and hugged his chest with softness and warmth. There were two changes of wool socks, a woolen shirt, and tough, denim trousers. She hadn't forgotten his heavy hunting jacket and a cap, and she had remembered warm gloves.

When he was dressed he was not only warm, but the stout clothing gave him the feeling of being armored against whatever the days or weeks ahead might bring. When he got into the pack it fitted snugly and balanced so perfectly he could move as though it were part of him, though he knew it must weigh close to forty pounds.

With his knife he cut a stout maple sapling, trimmed it so he might use it to walk with a forward cant, so the weight of the pack would be resting on his back instead of pulling against the shoulder straps.

Within the hour they were out of the forest. Russet used the hedgerows along Highway 67 to screen them from passing cars. They went around Dousman at around two-fifteen. There were only a few scattered lights in the homes. Then he swung back to parallel the highway, and it wasn't long when they came to where it intersected Highway 18. Russ went to his knees and pulled out of the pack to rest before attempting to cross. Gray lay off to the side and a little way behind him.

There had been a quickening of traffic shortly after one o'clock, a signal the taverns had closed. But now the highways were largely deserted. Russ gave himself five minutes and then, swinging into the pack, he ran across Highway 18. The wolf seemed reluctant to cross. Since leaving the forest he had become increasingly nervous. Finally, he dashed across with ears laid back and tail carried low.

It was almost dawn by the time they came to the Madison-Milwaukee freeway, and time to look for a hideout in which to spend the day. Russ paralleled the road until he came to a culvert. Staying in the shadows of the concrete abutment he went into the culvert, but Gray would not follow. It would have been an ideal place. There was even a puddle of water from which to drink, and no one would likely bother them because the freeway was closed to pedestrians.

He tried to coax the wolf into the shelter, but Gray only backed farther away. Russ scooped water with his hands to drink from the puddle and then went back out. He'd have to make a run for it across two lanes of pavement and the broad median strip. He hoped the wolf would follow.

Already commuters were going both directions — to Milwaukee and Madison — and cars whizzed by at irritating intervals. Finally, there came the moment when no headlights were in sight in either direction. Giving a low whistle, the boy ran up the green slope to the concrete. He hurried across and down the other side. He ran up the side of the next roadway and, crossing over, raced down and went to his knees in some marsh grass just as a pair of headlights came in sight.

Gray had not followed.

The car roared by, and then there was an intermittent flow of traffic, with shock waves of air coming all the way down on both sides of each lane. Russ felt the impact of pressure as two trucks went by and he knew that it was nearly enough to panic the wolf. He supposed he'd have to make a run for it — go back. He settled into his shoulder straps, got to his knees, and then raised himself into a sprinter's starting position.

But he didn't spring from the stance to make a dash because there was a screeching of tires being tortured by cement and then, in the headlights of a wildly swerving car, Russ saw the wolf and he only barely missed being hit.

"You darn fool!" the boy said, when the wolf came down to him. The wolf was trembling with fright so he quickly changed the tone of his voice. "It's okay, Gray. It's okay," and he tried to soothe the animal.

Russ only hoped the driver of the car hadn't recognized Gray for what he was — a wolf. He hoped the driver thought he had nearly struck a large, white dog, because if word got out they had left the forest, the search would be extended and their chances of going undetected would be far smaller.

"Come on! We have to get out of here," the boy said, getting up and striking straight north through the marsh to where a dark line of trees offered sanctuary.

It was a small tamarack stand and the trees, already bare of needles, looked as though they'd been swept by fire and were dead. Russ didn't like the feeling, though he was reluctant to go much further, because already the lights of Oconomowoc were a brightness in the sky ahead and he didn't want to bed down too close to the city.

The wolf had ceased trembling and was following along, seemingly more inclined now to turn over pack leadership to the boy and follow wherever he went. But Russ doubted that it was anything more than a temporary concession. Gray was still in his prime, and it wasn't in the nature of the animal to relinquish leadership. More than likely he'd assume command, nebulous as it was, once the specter of blinding headlights and screeching brakes retreated to some shadowy corner of his brain.

The tamaracks were thick, the ground boggy, and the going was slow. Russ paced himself to conserve strength should an emergency arise and there was the need for it. Then they came to a slow incline and, shortly, they were walking up and out of the tamaracks onto a knoll standing with maples, oaks, ash, and a few elms.

The high ground had not been grazed. There was sumac along one edge of the woodlot and a mixture of hazel, prickly ash, dogwood, and blackberries on the other three sides. There was a tiny trickle of water, obviously a feeder spring for the marsh, and they would need that. So, this is it, Russ thought. Here we stop for the day.

He slipped out of the pack and eased it to the ground. Only then he realized what a burden it had been. Without it he felt light enough to fly. He shook himself to get the good feeling of being free of the load, and then began a trip around the woodlot to look over the country.

He knew the marsh and the freeway were to the south so he went along the eastern edge. It was open fields for as far as he could see. He knew Highway 67 was in that direction — maybe two miles, he guessed.

To the north there were more fields and, a quarter-mile away, farm buildings loomed. It was all right. Russ couldn't think of any reason for a farmer to visit this parcel of land at this time of the year.

To the west were large, dense woodlots and more marsh. It was probably the area he should have chosen to hide in, but it was too late now to make a change.

He went back to the tiny spring and drank, and then stretched out on the ground with his head on the pack to rest. Off to the side the wolf stretched out and put his head down on his forepaws, but instead of closing his eyes, he kept looking intently at the boy.

"You still scared, Gray? Or are you only confused because you can't know what I'm thinking or where we're going? Or maybe — do you know?"

Russ sometimes felt that animals, particularly dogs, cats, wolves, and some of the primates had the power almost to read human minds. It was a farfetched theory and there was little supporting evidence in anything he'd read on animal behaviorism, but it was a feeling he sometimes got. For certain he knew they could smell when a man was angry, frightened, or just purely content.

Daylight was filtering through the branches of the trees, so the boy made another swing around the woodlot. This time, Gray stayed by the pack and it pleased Russ to see that, like a dog, the wolf was quickly adjusting to this nomad life and recognizing the pack as the focal point around which their lives would revolve — the home place.

Around the woodlot all seemed serene, so Russ went back and began unpacking. There was sausage and cheese, small tins of canned meat and canned fruit. There were loaves of bread compressed to one-fourth their size, but no food which would need fire to prepare it.

At the bottom of the pack, to his surprise, was his transistor radio. It had most surely been put there by his mother.

He spread the shelter-half and, turning on

the radio, heard the voice of Bill Hoeft with the morning farm report. He spread the contents of the pack on the triangle of canvas so he could make an assessment.

There was a tiny flashlight, plenty of matches, his wallet with fifty dollars in it, some rags, a length of rope, small first-aid kit, safety and straight pins, compass — mostly survival items, but some too which would make their days and nights more comfortable.

Sorting out food items he found three cans of dog food and was grateful for that, because he knew that feeding the wolf was going to be one of the hardest of all jobs.

Now that it was light and he could look the animal over, he saw the bullet hadn't entered Gray's body, but had cut a deep furrow in the chest.

"Boy, were you lucky," Russ said.

Gray looked at the boy with dull eyes. It was obvious he still had some fever, and it was also obvious he'd lost considerable weight.

"But I think you'll make it," the boy said, taking a can of dog food and cutting it open with his knife.

He had just put the food down and was backing away when Hoeft's voice, coming from the tiny radio, grabbed his attention:

"A sheriff's report this morning indicates that the Kettle Moraine wolf hunt may swing to an area north of the forest. Clinton B. Swayne, agricultural agent, this morning reported seeing what appeared to be a large white wolf crossing Highway I-94 just south of Oconomowoc.

"The sheriff's department is giving Swayne's report more than the usual attention since he has visited the kennels and had seen the wolf while it was kenneled there.

"Now to Les Leonard at the stockyards for the morning livestock report. Les?"

Russ went over to turn the radio down so it was just loud enough to hear if any further developments were reported.

What a frustrating development! Well, he was committed to this thing now, so it would only mean they'd have to be extra alert. Perhaps if the search parties turned up no evidence along the freeway, the main effort would continue in the forest and they'd have little to fear. Nevertheless, he planned an escape route, and decided they'd go west into the heavier cover if need be.

"They'll be coming this way for a look anyway," he said, looking over at the wolf. He saw how thin Gray's flanks were and how the eyes had sunk back into his skull. He didn't feel that Gray's condition was critical, but thought it might become so unless he got more nourishment.

"You have to eat," he said, and he opened the other two cans of food and fed them to the wolf. Then he made himself a cheese sandwich and, after eating it, drank from the spring. He put everything except the radio into the pack and buckled the straps. If he had to make a run for it he wanted to be ready.

It was a perfect autumn day. The air was so clear he could see a spider's shining strand high up in an oak. When it moved, small slivers of shine glinted off it — a marvelous rope made right out of a living thing, the spider's body.

Sounds carried a great distance. He could hear the hum of traffic along the freeway, a rooster bragging over at the farmhouse, a dog barking down near Highway 67, a tractor growling on some far field.

Russ knew he should sleep if they were going to travel that night, but he was too keyed up to close his eyes and drift off. Gray was sleeping, a fitful sleep obviously rampant with wild dreams.

Perhaps, in his brain, the car lights were

bearing down on him and the tires were screeching and he could smell the burning rubber. Perhaps he was caught in the cone of searchlights and the guns were banging and the slug was tearing into his chest.

The wolf's muscles twitched spasmodically and, from time to time, his flews curled back to show the long, white teeth. Russ would have liked to move over and put a hand on the animal to reassure him and quiet the turmoil. Once, he did get up and move a few paces closer, but instantly the wolf was awake and his eyes were almost accusing.

Russ went back to lie down with his head on the pack. He regretted the impulse. It would never do to have the wolf mistrust him. He had to observe Gray's rules. He had to respect the wolf's desire to maintain a buffer area around himself. The critical distance was apparently ten feet. Come closer and Gray at once became restive and started to back off.

Wolves and dogs, particularly among strangers, observed strict rules of approach. Come closer, cross the invisible line, and precipitate a fight.

Russ couldn't bring himself to believe the wolf would attack. He was sure it was the animal's way of conveying to him, the boy, that freedom was a precious thing which Gray would under no circumstances relinquish, even if he had to run away or die to prove it.

There had been no further news of the wolf hunt so Russ turned the radio off to save the batteries. Sunshine seeping down through the trees warmed him. A few flies, having survived the frost, traced lazy flight circles around the dried blood that matted the wolf's hide. It was peaceful there on the knoll, and Russ felt lethargy weight his arms and legs and creep comfortably in waves of warmth into his mind. His eyes grew heavy and he was glad to give in and go to sleep.

The sun crested. Looking almost straight down it shone with the same benevolence on hunter and hunted alike. And, if there was consternation among the frustrated posse members combing the Kettle Moraine, there was quiet and peace for the two fugitives.

Of course, it couldn't last, but it was midafternoon before something — a whine from Gray or perhaps a skip in the beat of traffic along the freeway — awakened Russ. He looked at once toward the wolf. Gray was alert. His ears were erect to catch sound, his ruff bristling. He turned his head from side to side searching for some message on the air.

Russ listened, but there was nothing. Yet he was not deceived. Something had awakened him. Well, if they were coming he wasn't about to get caught lying there. Getting to his feet he hurried down into the tamaracks and coming through the bogs to the edge of the marsh looked out on the freeway.

The posse was there! At least a dozen cars with a police car fore and aft, with red lights flashing so freeway travelers wouldn't crash into the caravan.

Men were pouring out of the cars and assembling in the ditch. All had guns. While they stood talking, four broke away from the main group and went to examine the culvert which underpassed the highway.

Russ was glad they were not in it. It had been like a wolf to refuse such shelter. Wolves hated to be bottled up. They wanted to be able to jump in any direction which might seem necessary.

He waited until the posse crossed the fence and formed a long line before retreating. Then he went swiftly through the tamaracks and came up the knoll. Gray had not moved.

"Looks like they're coming," the boy said. The wolf had obviously smelled the men. He was on his feet and his eyes had narrowed and his ears had gone flat back.

Russ didn't want to run and expose themselves if that weren't necessary; but he had to know what direction the posse was taking, and he had to know when they were too close for them to comfortably remain where they were.

He looked at the oak under which they'd been sleeping, and then jumped for the lowest branch and pulled himself into the tree. With the agility of a squirrel he went up until he was high enough to look out over the tamaracks. He could see the posse. It was sweeping the marsh from east to west, right up to the edge of the tamarack woodlot, but in the direction of the thicker and more numerous woodlots to the west.

Russ saw at once that it was the logical direction for a posse to move. In fact, if he had come on this piece of country during daylight, it is likely he would have chosen the thicker woodlots to the west instead of the isolated island of trees to which, in darkness, they had come.

Well, a guy had to get lucky once in a while.

9

NEXT MORNING GRAY was hungry. Russ gave him some cheese and sausage. Feeding the wolf would be as much a problem as evading pursuit. Except for the three cans of dog food which had already been consumed, there was nothing for Gray. Weight had obviously been a deterrent to packing otherwise. So Russ figured to share when necessary and hunt when possible.

They had walked all the preceding night, and by dawn they had come to the heart of Wisconsin's dairyland. Hedgerows were sparse, woodlots infrequent. So, at the first graying light, Russ had turned from the railroad tracks they were walking to climb a hill which lifted high enough to give him visual command of the country all around. From the top where they lay, he could see far down and out across checkerboard fields of golden stubble and bright green fields of winter wheat, and he felt like an eagle must in his aerie and only wished he and the wolf might soar and fly away like the great birds.

Their hill was alfalfa, frostbitten but still green, and though there wasn't a stick or stone to hide behind, they needed none. They were high enough. Should an intruder come up one side of the hill they could slip down the other and be off and away.

On the previous day the posse had concentrated on the woodlots to the west of them, passing up their isolated hideout, and then at dusk they had given up the chase.

The boy and the wolf, leaving as soon as it had been dark, circled Oconomowoc and on coming to the tracks took them northwest. Except for a few farms they were out of the main flow of traffic. Only once, when a train with its wildly swinging light and roaring engine came bearing down on them, did the wolf panic. Russ had crouched low until the train had swept past with a wash of wild weed-bending.

Gray had bolted, and it was a half-hour before he came back. But he would not come up on the grade to walk the roadbed and, instead, stayed off to the side in the low cover.

But they had made good time and, walking for ten hours with infrequent rests, Russ figured they had come perhaps thirty-five miles. His cross-country training was paying off. Even with the heavy pack, he was able to move at what he guessed was a speed of three and one-half miles an hour without tiring.

But though the land was fertile, thrifty farmers had left little cover for game, and the only bird which appreciated the landowner's economies was the Hungarian partridge. They had put up two coveys while climbing the hill, and now another had landed two hundred feet in front of where they were stretched out in the alfalfa.

Russ guessed the partridge were feeding on grasshoppers. The insects would be lethargic, some perhaps even dead from the frost, and the birds would have easy picking. From time to time Russ could see the tiny head of a sentinel bird rise above the alfalfa tops, and in this way he kept track of the covey.

"What do you think, Gray?" he asked the wolf. "They'll sit awfully tight. Wait until the last second."

The wolf had seen the birds. Perhaps he even smelled them too. His tongue was lolling and a tiny drop of moisture was beaded at the pink end of it.

Getting up, Russ circled so the wind was blowing directly from the birds to them. When the scent impact hit the wolf he dropped to a crouch. Then the boy hurriedly circled until he was opposite Gray.

"Okay, Gray, let's move in." Whether or not the wolf understood the boy, he began a slow, low sneak to where the birds were huddled.

Russ got down to his hands and knees too, hoping the sentinel bird would again lift its head so he could determine the precise location of the covey. It did. The tiny head, beadlike eyes bright, popped up and as quickly disappeared. They had the covey directly between them.

Gray had dropped almost to his belly. The boy did likewise. Inch by careful inch. Foot by foot, to close the trap.

"Sit tight, little birds," Russ prayed to himself. "Wait a little longer, pretty birds. Don't be frightened. Don't fly."

Russ raised a little. He stared intently at the spot where the sleek little head had been raised. There was the bird. In spite of the camouflage, his eyes had sorted things out. He saw it! Burnt orange and gray and compact and waiting. Then, more birds holding flat and tight to the ground came into focus. They were grouped, huddled, almost as close as quail will group while roosting in a marsh. Twenty, maybe twenty-five and that was a lot of birds, so maybe they'd get one or two.

Russ looked to the wolf. His eyes were mere slits. His ears were flat. His ruff lay back. His tail was stretched out behind and it was a miracle of movement that he could slither so adroitly along without lifting.

When the boy was within a half-dozen feet of the huddled covey he lifted slowly to a sprinter's crouch. Then, as though boy and wolf had arranged some signal, both leaped forward. Russ could hear Gray's jaws snapping. He flailed his arms into the rising flock, and feathers flew.

It was over in seconds. Birds had exploded in all directions and were already distant specks far down the hill where the fields stretched flat. But there were three birds on the ground and a winged one was hurrying away to hide. Gray was on it before it got ten feet.

Russ collected the three dead birds, and with Gray carrying the one he had caught they went back to the top of the hill. The wolf lay down with his partridge between his paws. Taking out his knife, Russ split the skin along the breastbone and peeled each bird right out of its feathers.

He put the three carcasses together off to one side, and then took sausage from the pack and cut himself a slice. He sat down to eat and, when he took the first bite, Gray picked up his partridge, flattened it with a single crunch, and swallowed it whole. Then he moved over to where the other birds were lying and repeated the performance.

Russ would never have believed it possible if he hadn't once seen a Labrador retriever do the same thing with quail. He and his father had stumbled on a covey while floating a river to shoot ducks. They had killed four quail. On the way home they put the little birds and the ducks in the back of the station wagon with the dog. He had turned just in time to see Ace swallow the last quail — legs, head, wings, feathers, and all.

Refreshed, Russ lay back and Gray began to clean himself. It was a good sign. The wolf, plagued by fever and pain, had let himself go. His white hide was streaked with dirt. He was full of burrs and bootjack sticktights. The hair puckered in places as though he were a stuffed wolf with the stuffing coming out.

But now his nose was no longer dry and pitted but once again glistening black, moist and quick to quiver at every errant breeze.

He started at the tail pulling out burrs with his teeth. After the burrs were out, he slicked the hairs of the tail with his wet, pink tongue. Tail clean, he started on his legs, and then went after the dried blood on his chest.

Russ fell asleep while watching the wolf and when he awakened it was to see a new, slick, and glistening Gray sleeping quietly, muzzle on outstretched paws.

The boy looked at his watch. It was exactly noon. He turned on the radio. There was five minutes of nationwide news, mostly about the war and about students demonstrating at an eastern university. The report reminded him of all the school he was missing, and he wondered how he'd ever be able to make it up. Only at the end of the report did the announcer mention the hunt:

"Searchers are still combing the Kettle

Moraine Forest just west of here for the wolf which escaped from the Clagg Kennels and for the body of the boy authorities believe the wolf killed.

"Some searchers say they will never find the remains of the youth, Russet Clagg, son of the kennel owner, because what the wolf hasn't eaten he has buried. Others say the surmise is ridiculous, that the wolf would not bury the body.

"Meanwhile, reports are coming in from other parts of the state. Fishermen as far west as Prairie du Chien have reported seeing the wolf along the Mississippi River while hunters have said they've seen the wolf as far as the forests north of Antigo. If it is the wolf, obviously he has grown wings.

"That's the news for today, and now for the weather. . . ."

Russ clicked the radio off. Whatever the weather, they'd wait for it.

Far below, a farmer was driving a herd of black and white cattle. They came down a lane and through a gate into one of the huge fields which stretched all the way up the hill to where they lay. Russ didn't figure the cows would bother to climb the hill. There was plenty of forage along the level. The farmer closed the gate and went back down the lane toward a stand of trees which hid the house and barn.

Russ liked the hill he had chosen. He felt safe up there so high above everything. To the east a quarter-mile and far below was their escape route, the railroad tracks. Twice during the morning, trains, looking like toys, had passed north.

It would have been something if he had been able to get Gray into an empty boxcar so they could ride right out of the danger zone. He had thought about it, but didn't bother to give it really serious consideration. Gray wouldn't go near the tracks, much less approach a boxcar.

Well, so they'd walk. If Russ hadn't skipped any days he figured it was October eighth. There might be some days of cold and even snow, but winter was still a month or more away. They had time. In a month, thirty days, they could cover lots of territory — hundreds of miles.

Of course, there was the problem of keeping full stomachs. Russ estimated he could get by with what was in the pack for a week, but he'd have to find something for Gray, if not every day, then every second day for sure.

A wolf could go a long time between meals.

He had read somewhere that biologists had determined they could live eighteen days without eating anything before starving to death. Eighteen days was a long time, but Russ didn't believe Gray could last that long — not at the rate they'd be traveling.

He got out the map and, spreading it on the sweet-smelling alfalfa, considered all the possible routes. Then he ate a piece of sausage and napped, and when he awakened the sun was gone and shadows were bringing the night up to where they lay.

10

For four days of perfect Indian summer they followed the tracks. Where westbound rails intersected tracks heading north they turned so the North Star was always in their eyes. Every night, while they'd walked, there'd been stars and at least a piece of moon, and the days, when they'd rested, had been golden with meltingly warm sunshine.

A few stray dogs had come close enough to sniff, but turned tail when Gray had bristled. And every day reports of the hunt on the radio became less frequent and of shorter duration. The search for them seemed to be tapering off.

They walked around the city of Watertown and many smaller towns including Clyman, Juneau, Burnett, Atwater, until they were just south of Waupun and right on the edge of the Horicon National Wildlife Refuge.

In their day camp, on a small peninsula right in the heart of the marsh (where Russ was almost sure no one would come to bother them because trespassing was illegal), they were surrounded by such a myriad of birds as visit few other places.

The incessant chattering of blackbirds, chanting of geese, chipping of southbound warblers, quacking of mallards, made sleep impossible. But Russ didn't care because he felt an affinity for the place, a special closeness to it, and here he would have liked to linger except that on the fourteenth, two days hence, this wildlife paradise would be turned into a purgatory.

The waterfowl hunting season opened on that day and he wanted to be far north before thousands of hunters converged on the area to gun for Canada geese.

He had hunted the marsh once and had no desire to ever do so again. It had not been hunting, but calculated murder, with gunners forming firing lines which extended from the refuge perimeter far back into the surrounding countryside.

What's more, they were out of food. Unable to catch or stone or trap or dig out any living thing, Russ had been forced to share his rations with the wolf, and now they were hungry.

It was ironic they should be without food when the marsh teemed with it. Russ was sure, if the wolf had come to this place on his own, he would have been able to survive. There were deer in the willow brakes, raccoons on the islands, cottontails, opossums, mink, muskrats, weasels, mice — all manner of wild things.

But for some reason Gray made no move to hunt. Perhaps if the pinch of hunger had turned into the pangs of starvation the wolf might have left his clumsy, two-footed companion, and foraged for himself. But except for a dozen or so field mice he had picked up as he walked along, Gray had not tried to hunt by himself.

Russ was fearful of permitting the wolf to get too hungry. Extreme hunger could be a dangerous thing for both. They would take unnecessary chances and at a time when they were the least physically and mentally able to cope with hazards.

The knoll they were on was grassy except

for a few scrub oak still cloaked in brown dry leaves, and it was surrounded on three sides by water. Always there were gallinules and coots pulling tendrils up from the mud, and goose families of two adults and several grown youngsters often swam so close he could see their glistening white cheek patches.

A goose would have made a feast for both of them. He'd even risk a fire if there were goose breasts to brown over the hot coals.

But the geese, though they came close, were not foolish enough to swim within range of an attack.

Indians, some historians claimed, had sometimes gotten them by swimming underwater and getting a leg hold. Some trick, Russ thought, if you could do it. They used hollow reeds, according to tales he'd read, for breathing tubes to get into the flocks.

Russ had only half believed the stories, though perhaps they were true. Maybe he should give it a try. The sun was warm. He had the whole day. It wasn't likely anyone would trespass onto the refuge to bother them.

He got up and went down to feel the water. It was icy. He walked back up the slope and lay down again. Gray, accustomed by now to their nocturnal walks and daytime camps, had curled into a ball and was sound asleep. When the boy moved he uncurled enough to watch, but when Russ sat down he closed his eyes again.

"Gray, we have to eat, and what have I got to lose," Russ said. The wolf's ears twitched, but he did not open his eyes.

"If we don't eat today we're going to be starving by tomorrow and I'm here to tell you neither of us is going to travel far on an empty belly."

He got up again and walked to a patch of pencil reeds. Cutting one off at the water's surface, he brought it back to the knoll. He cut off the tip and tried breathing through it. He could get some air, but not very much, so he took a long stem of tough grass and pushed it like a pipe cleaner all the way through the reed. He put his lips to the reed and tried again. It worked.

Well, why not? He pulled off his bird shooters and socks and slipped out of his denims. Then he stripped bare and, shivering a little, walked down the bank, and slipping into the icy water, waded out.

The water was chest-deep and the bottom was mucky. Two hundred feet ahead was a flotilla of Canadas — families grouped into a flock. He crouched until only his head was above the waterline and began a slow stalk.

The icy water numbed his feet and hands and put such a crush of coldness across his chest he had difficulty breathing. But he didn't turn back, and the Canadas let him get to within fifty feet before they showed signs of becoming restless. Putting the reed in his mouth he submerged. When he tried to breathe he sucked water into his nostrils and came up choking and sputtering.

The geese, heads high now, drifted their flock away. He held his nose with his right hand and the reed with the other and went under again. This time he could get air into his lungs without sucking water.

He tried opening his eyes. The water stung. He closed them. He'd get closer before opening them again. Slowly, then, he inched along with his little green lifeline making a barely perceptible ripple.

After a minute he opened his eyes. The world around was gray-green. There were floating specks, obviously duckwort, stems of rush clumps, and one mud minnow which darted away and dived to the bottom in a cloud of mud when he winked an eye. But he could see no geese.

Perhaps the flock had moved. Though shivering, he hated to surface and spoil his chances. He moved again, slowly forward, and now it took a positive effort of his will to stay submerged.

But he would, he told himself. He'd stay under. There was such a thing as making yourself go through with a project, and he meant to do this thing now that he had come this far.

After another minute he opened his eyes to the hazy gray-green world of water. At once he saw webbed feet lazily waving backward and forward. It was like looking at a motion picture in slow motion. The geese were not more than ten feet away and, judging by the number of feet, there must have been a dozen birds. He was close enough to see the tiny claws at the ends of their toes and the tiny callouses on the bottoms of their webs.

After resting, he began again to walk, slowly — one foot forward and into the mud and then carefully the other foot forward to come down beside the first — another inch, another foot, another yard.

If the geese knew he was down there they gave no indication. He could see their gray bottoms now, sleek as canvas. Another step. One more. Then he lunged and had a leg. At the same time he burst up out of the water into the middle of the goose flock.

The effect on the geese was the same as if he'd dropped a bomb among them. They exploded in every direction and their honking was a riotous clamor which sent birds into the air in every direction.

But he had no time for any except the gander he'd gotten a hand hold on. If he had thought catching a goose was going to be difficult, he hadn't reckoned on how difficult it might be to hold onto one.

The bird he had hold of was an adult of perhaps twelve pounds, with wing elbows hard and driving as sledge hammers, and a bonelike beak which it kept spearing straight at his eyes. He covered his face with his free hand and held fast to the leg with the other, while the bird lifted and fell back, hammering his head and neck and shoulders in a frenzy for its freedom.

The bird was too strong. Perhaps on land where he'd have the advantage of better footing, but never here in water nearly shoulder deep could he hope to hold it. Leaving his face unprotected he made several unsuccessful grabs for the other leg, but in the end he had to relinquish his hold. The bird went off on a slant, hit the water, skidded back into the air, and with a wild winging went high, bugling all the while about its injured pride.

Russ stood deflated. Blood was running from a cut on his cheek and several on his right arm. His ears were ringing from the repeated hammerlike blows of the wing elbows. He had known Canadas were strong. He'd seen captive birds drive a dog right out of the yard. But he hadn't anticipated such fury.

Back on shore, Gray watched with open curiosity as he came naked from the water limping a little now over the sharp stones as though his feet and legs had to somehow lend their sympathy to the rest of his body.

Looking back out over the marsh, he saw the ruckus had put up geese, ducks, and blackbirds in every direction. He hoped the swirl of birds wouldn't bring a Federal warden down into the marsh to investigate.

Using the palms of his hands he sluiced water off his body before crawling back into his long underwear. It was a comfort.

By the time he had dressed, there was no sun, and, in the west, storm clouds were gathering. He had been waiting for it. He knew the weather had been too balmy, too good to last.

Now he had to sleep if he wanted to travel that night. He lay back in the grass and looked out over the marsh. Birds were settling back among the rushes everywhere, but around the little peninsula he and Gray were on, there was a buffer zone of inactivity. The word had gone out:

"There is danger there! Back by the trees. Next to the shore."

Russ believed in this sort of communication even between species, and here was another instance of it. Not even a coot swam within a hundred yards of where the boy and the wolf were lying.

Sleep wouldn't come, try hard as he would, and even Gray seemed restless. Far to the west clouds were piling hill upon hill of black trouble and, intermittently, he felt tremors in the earth as thunder grumbled.

Russ had no fear of storms. He knew that he and the wolf could survive the worst, providing they had full stomachs. It was only when a man was hungry and weakening that his mind and body couldn't cope with rain, wind, snow, or sleet.

Neither he nor the wolf had weakened as yet, but he had been forced to pull his belt up a couple notches and the wolf looked lean, because they'd been on half-rations and all day there had been nothing.

The ideal way would have been to camp right where they were and put out snares of twine and wire, build deadfalls — set traps for small game — and then scout the backwaters for landlocked fish. But by tomorrow at this time the hunters would be scouting the area for blinds from which to shoot, and if there was one place they didn't want to be, it was among a horde of armed men.

As soon as it was dark Russ got up and started out of the refuge. Lightning was flashing in jagged thrusts. Thunder boomed and the echoes rolled back and forth across the earth. The rain had come abruptly in a thrust of water from the west. They had to lower their heads to walk into it.

Back on the tracks they could turn north to move toward the lights of Waupun, Wisconsin's prison city. The tracks went east of town and, where they crossed Highway 49 which bisected the northern end of the refuge, Russ went into a grove of trees and swinging out of his pack tossed it to the ground.

"I'm going into town," he said, turning to the wolf. "You'd best wait here."

Gray followed the boy until they were within range of street lights and then turned back toward the grove where the pack lay. By the time he reached the city limits, Russ was soaked. Several cars had whisked by, but he had stepped off into the shadows as each bore down on him.

Where the sidewalk began he put his head down and hurried, hoping anyone he met might see just another boy anxious to get home and out of the rain.

Lights were on in all the houses he passed, and through the glistening rain-streaked windows he could see people moving about. The glimpses of domestic warmth and plenty and peace hit him hard, and he suddenly wished he were home on the davenport wrapped in his woolly robe watching television or reading or just looking to see what patterns the raindrops were painting on the panes.

People sure took a lot for granted, he thought. Being safe and warm was such a routine thing few people ever thought enough about it to consider it a blessing. He shivered. What he wouldn't give to sit at his place at the table knowing Gray was secure and warm and well fed just outside.

He was almost downtown before he came to a little corner store and went in. Steam lifted from his wet clothes and his boots made a sucking sound. Water dripped from the bill of his cap and, when he stood by the counter, a pool of water began to spread on the floor below.

"Boy, you're soaked," a voice said. Russ looked up into the face of a middle-aged, dark-haired woman.

He forced a laugh. "Yeah, I got caught in the rain. My father's car stalled."

"What can I do for you?" the woman asked.

Russ ordered two loaves of bread, cheese, sausage, cans of tinned meat and fruit, and a dozen chocolate bars. It filled a brown bag.

"Do you have any dog food?"

"Dry or canned?"

Russ thought a moment and then said: "Dry."

"I've got this," the woman pointed to five-pound bags.

"I'll take one. No wait, better make it two."

He handed her two ten-dollar bills and she gave him change. Then, with the bag of groceries under one arm and the two five-pound bags of dog food under the other, he went back out into the rain.

"Better hurry," the woman called out after him, "looks like it's going to be an all-nighter."

Anyway, they'd eat, Russ thought. He

turned east and hurried along the sidewalk. He crossed an intersection and there before him was a yellow phone booth, open and inviting. He put the groceries and dog food against the east side of the booth out of the rain and went in. Putting in his dime, he dialed the long distance operator.

"Number, please."

"414-662-2864 collect."

"And who is calling, please?"

Russ hesitated. He had forgotten that he would have to give his name. He didn't dare. The operator might recognize it since it had been in the newspapers and on television and radio so much of late.

"Are you there?" the operator asked.

"Yes. My name is Gray Russet."

"Thank you." He heard the operator dial. He hoped whoever answered would get the combination of names, his and the wolf's, and know that he was calling.

There was a voice. It was his father's. "I have a collect call from Waupun, Wisconsin, from a Mr. Gray Russet. Will you accept the charges?"

There was a moment of silence. Then the voice said: "Put him on."

"Dad! Hi. How are you? How's Mom?"

"Fine. Just fine." He could hear his father

trying to keep his voice under control. "And you?" the father asked.

"Doing okay, Dad. Really okay. Walking the rails mostly."

"Good idea. Good idea."

"Any people around, Dad?"

"Well, yes there are."

"Okay, I won't talk too much."

"That's right. That's right. But wait. Here's Mrs. Clagg."

Russ waited. Then he heard his mother's voice. It was questioning: "Yes? Hello?"

"Mom!"

"Oh!"

"Everything is all right, Mom."

There was a pause. He knew she would be struggling with her emotions. Finally: "I'm glad to hear that."

"I just called to tell you not to worry."

"We won't. We know you understand what you're doing."

They were both silent again. Russ couldn't think of anything more to say. Finally, in a low voice, he said: "Mom, it's okay. Believe me. Everything is all right."

Then he hung up and stood there in the cold phone booth with the rain splatting against the glass and felt warm tears on his cheeks.

11

ONCE OUTSIDE the city limits, Russ broke into a lope. The bags were getting soaked by the rain and he was afraid they might fall apart. He kept his head down, and though some cars whisked by, he attracted no attention. When he came into the grove of trees, he slowed to a walk so as not to frighten the wolf.

It took him a while to bring objects into focus in the pelting rain, and then he saw Gray, off to one side, waiting.

"We eat," he said, and taking a bag of dog food he tore it open and dumped the five pounds into a pile on the ground. Then he put all except some bread and cheese and sausage into the pack, and wrapping the shelter-half around the remaining five pounds of dog food, leaned against the east side of a tree and ate slowly.

Gray ate the five pounds of food swiftly and was through before Russ finished. The wolf walked out of the grove to the roadside and lapped water from the ditch. Swallowing the last piece of bread, Russ followed and, kneeling beside the puddle, scooped up water with both hands. Then, bellies bulging, they headed into the rain, turned north at the tracks, and walked.

The rain was relentless. The boy, head bent and leaning a little forward, guided on a rail to keep from stumbling. The wolf, tail tucked and ears flat, bucked the wet brush alongside the tracks.

It was midnight when they came to Brandon. Russ was thoroughly soaked and the cold was biting down until it seemed to be drilling right through his bones into the marrow. Another wave of homesickness swept over him as they swung around the village. He had an uncle living in Brandon, a completely warm and enthusiastic uncle who took him fishing in nearby lakes and in the evening always gave him a hot drink before going to bed. What he'd have given now for that warming drink and the soft bed!

Ripon was next. It was a small city, but a lively one, and the boy planned to make their camp before they got there and then circle it during the next night.

The rain stopped just at dawn, and they made camp two miles south of Ripon. Soaked already, they waded right into a small slough and walked out to a tiny island. The slough was too small to hold ducks and geese, and hunters weren't likely to come, so the boy risked a fire and, lying close, let his clothes dry on his body while Gray cleaned himself with his tongue.

That night he gave Gray half of the remaining dog food and treated himself to canned fruit, two tins of meat, and a half-loaf of bread. Like an animal, he was learning to live on one meal a day and was pleased to discover that such a routine seemed acceptable to his needs.

North of Ripon at Rush Lake, the railroad bisected with one roadbed aiming northwest and ending after a little way at the city of Berlin, and the other apparently crossing Lake Poygan and then, after a dogleg, heading straight north again.

During the night they passed around Rush Lake, went right through Waukau, and ended up by morning just south of Lake Poygan. Now Russ figured they were one hundred miles north of the Kettle Moraine Forest, though their circuitous route had probably cost them an extra fifty miles of walking.

They camped that day in a woodlot right alongside the railroad. Gray ate the last of the dog food and both slept well.

That night they crossed the big lake, with Gray refusing to walk the trestle bridge and swimming the narrows instead. Now Oshkosh was south of them and already the woodlots were larger and there were more pines than deciduous trees. Even the air had a different feel and taste to it as the webbing of industrial cities was left behind and they moved into the near north country of tiny towns, rushing rivers, thousands of lakes, and soon — very soon! — endless mile on mile of forests.

So the days and the nights and the landmarks slipped away: Allenville, Larsen, Medina, Hortonville, New London, Sugar Bush, Bear Creek, Clintonville, Marion, Split Rock — and then the wolf needed food, and he needed it badly. The remaining rations would sustain him, the boy, for a while, but there wasn't enough for Gray.

They were just south of Tigerton in a small forest which bordered on some farmlands. In a pocket of low ground, the boy had seen the first snowshoe hares of the trip. They were mottled, on their way to becoming white for the winter.

He had been sitting on the edge of the pocket trying to think of some way to bag one or two of the hares when Gray's head went up and his nose started to twitch. Russ watched him closely to see if it was dinner or danger the wolf scented.

When the wolf's ears stayed erect and his ruff failed to bristle, Russ surmised it must be game. The wolf started forward at a swift trot and the boy followed. Before he'd gone a hundred steps, Russ could hear a threshing in the brush and he had to run to keep the wolf in sight.

When the boy broke into a clearing, Gray was already finishing off a yearling calf which had all but throttled itself in a fence.

His first feeling was one of relief that the wolf once again had meat. Then, quickly, he recognized the jeopardy such a thing as calf killing might put them in by attracting attention to their presence in the area.

Maybe if Gray didn't eat at the carcass but let it lie . . . He walked toward the animal. "Let's leave it," he said. "Then they might think dogs finished it off."

But Gray had both paws possessively over the calf's neck, and there was blood on his bib and on his muzzle.

Perhaps if he left, Gray might follow. He turned and walked into the woods. Then he stood and waited. The wolf did not come. He went back. Gray had moved around and ripped open the calf's belly and was eating. Steam lifted from the warm entrails, and Russ felt a little sick.

There was nothing he could do, so he went back to the marsh pocket where he'd seen the hares and where he'd left his pack and settled down to wait.

Within an hour the wolf was back and, with sides bulging, he lay down and began the long task of cleaning himself.

That night when Russ got ready to move out, the wolf refused to follow.

"But it's dangerous here. That calf is going to be missed and then they'll come looking."

When Gray wouldn't follow, the boy went to the tracks and began walking. He went a mile, almost to the outskirts of Tigerton, but the wolf didn't come.

He waited a half-hour, an hour, and then went back. Gray was where he'd left him in the marshy pocket of the little forest.

"Gray, this is suicide," the boy pleaded.

Twice more that night the boy left, hoping the wolf would follow. Then he gave up and, just before dawn, Gray went back to the carcass to feed again. When he finished he came back to the marsh pocket to sleep.

A boy and a man came looking for the calf shortly after sunrise. Gray hugged the ground when he first heard their voices and then, getting up, slunk off deeper into the forest. Russ remained where he was, ready if need be, to retreat.

The boy found the calf. "Here, Dad! My gosh!"

"What's the matter?" the father shouted, and Russ could hear him running. There was silence.

"Coyotes likely," he heard the father, "but I haven't seen any sign. Might have been dogs," Russ felt relieved.

There was silence again as the two obviously examined the mutilated carcass. Then he heard the father's voice: "I don't suppose it'd do any good to go to Marion and get Paul Merkle's hounds. The trail is probably cold by now."

"We could try!" There was eagerness in the boy's voice.

"No time. Right now with corn still standing I just don't have time to be going off on a wild goose chase."

Russ breathed more easily. He didn't want to have to run out front of dogs. Not in strange country. In the Kettle Moraine Forest he always felt he had a chance because he knew the lay of the land, but here . . .

The voices receded. Russ lay back and put his head on the pack. Gradually, he felt his muscles smooth out. Slowly he relaxed.

Gray was a long time coming back, and now he lay with his head high and constantly alert.

"Well, you asked for it," the boy said. "Now when it gets dark I hope you have the good sense to get out of here."

During the afternoon Russ napped. The day was just turning gray when voices awakened him. The boy and his father were coming, so he decided to move.

Gray followed willingly through the dim forest, and soon they were back out on the tracks and it was dark.

Russ hoped to get past Tigerton, Whitcomb, Wittenberg, and just past Eland where he knew from the map the road divided again with one spur going northwest to Wausau and the other line continuing straight on.

He wanted no part of the Wausau route. Here the rails came near the heavily traveled Highway 51, and there were too many towns, too many people.

They had no trouble getting around Tigerton and, once the city was bypassed, Russ leaned into the pack straps and, lengthening his stride, started to make miles.

The walking was toughening him as the cross-country running never had. But that was understandable. He was walking ten and twelve hours a day, while his cross-country training had been confined to two hours a day and only five days a week.

He felt heartened as he walked. The calf killing had been a close call, but now he could put it out of his mind, and he hummed a tune just under his breath so he'd have a rhythm, a beat to put each boot down to. It was easier that way. He always hummed softly, even when he ran. You could pace yourself with a tune — fast or slow, but always steady.

What's more, walking or running to a tune made the time slip away. It had an almost hypnotic effect and the miles melted behind.

With the tune in his mind, and his eyes on the rails, Russ kept moving north without realizing the wolf had left him. He first felt it when the toe of a boot hit a stone and he stumbled, breaking the rhythm. He stopped abruptly and turned. There was no white wolf among the railside weeds.

He turned, whistled softly, and waited. Then he went south several hundred yards hoping to find Gray had perhaps come across a crippled cottontail, a nest of mice, or an injured bird. But there was no sign of the wolf.

Gray wasn't going to take a chance on becoming hungry again. He was headed back to the carcass of the calf.

Russ held his watch so the light of the stars illuminated the hands. It was nearly midnight. Perhaps the wolf was already feeding. Maybe he should wait. He couldn't chance it, so he retraced his steps. But now there was no tune humming up from his throat, only the taste of fear on his tongue, the sour taste of a stomach upset by a premonition that some great danger was about to threaten them.

Finding the forest was easy, but getting back to the marshy pocket where they'd had their day camp was difficult. He had to make four separate thrusts into the forest before he hit upon it, and by then it was past two o'clock in the morning.

He would have stopped to rest except that a strange jangling — as of chains — startled him just as he was about to sit down.

He moved carefully, quietly. The little moon there was had not yet risen so he had only the light of the stars, but the many nights of moving about in the dark had given him some extra perceptive ability and he moved easily around obstacles.

At the edge of the forest, he paused and dropped to one knee. Gray was out there by the carcass. He could see him dimly white. Russ whistled softly. The wolf did not come. He got up and started toward the animal, and when Gray backed off, he again heard the jangle of a chain.

Then it hit him. A *trap!* The farmer had set a trap at the carcass and the wolf had blundered into it.

Now, he had his work cut out for him. How did you get a wolf out of a trap? A wolf who refused to be touched even during such intimacy as their flight had made inevitable?

Taking a dog out of a trap was trouble enough. There'd been a German shepherd, a blue ribbon obedience champion, and the dog had been ready to tear him to pieces every time he got close. He'd finally been forced to go all the way back home to get a huge canvas to throw over the animal so he could pull the trapped leg out without getting chewed up.

Still he had to try. So, putting down his pack, he moved in. Gray backed off as far as the chain would permit and, crouching low with his ears flat, lifted his lips so his teeth showed.

"Gray, I'm only going to help. I want to help." Then, he almost had to laugh at himself for sounding so silly.

He backed off and looked at his watch. It was nearly two-thirty. It would start to get light at six-thirty. That gave him four hours. It sounded like a lot of time, but even if he got the wolf out of the trap, he knew they'd have to put miles between them and this place just in case the farmer decided to get dogs and take up the chase.

He tried to approach the wolf again and wondered if he should risk getting bitten. Perhaps, after all, Gray would not bite. They'd been together for so many years. But then he remembered the German shepherd and one of the cats he'd taken from a musk-rat trap. She had just about torn his hands off when he tried to free her.

Finally, he sat down to think about it and in the end he knew he couldn't risk being bitten. If it was a serious wound that would definitely be the end for both of them. Then he'd be forced to go for help and leave the wolf to shift for himself. The hunt for Gray would be resumed within hours. They'd get him.

Well, what else?

He leaned forward. Now that his eyes had become accustomed to the scene, he could pick out details. The trap was nailed to a log much too heavy for him to carry any distance. The chain between log and wolf was perhaps six, maybe seven feet. If he got to the log he'd be closer than the wolf had yet permitted.

Yet, it was the only way. Taking out his knife and unclasping the long blade, he moved toward the trap toggle. Gray backed so far his tail came high into the air and his head close to the ground with the front paw held by the trap stretched far out in front.

"Easy, Boy. Easy. I'm not going to hurt you."

Ten feet. That was the critical distance. Gray's teeth were whiter even than his white muzzle.

"Easy now. Easy. Easy."

He was beside the log. For a moment he crouched watching the wolf. Then he began digging with his knife blade at the huge staple which had been used to make the chain fast.

As he dug he could smell creosote. The farmer had stapled the trap to a part of a railroad tie. The knife brought the wood away in long splinters. When he had a trench gouged on either side of the staple, he took hold of the chain and pulled. The staple came free of the tie, and Russ backed slowly away without getting to his feet.

When he was fifteen feet from the wolf he got up and started walking toward the forest. Gray did not follow. When he'd gone a little way among the trees he gave a low whistle, and then he heard the chain and knew the wolf was moving. He went back to the marshy pocket and lay down to wait. The sounds of the wolf's progress was clearly audible. The chain made a jangling sound as it caught on the brush and snapped free, and Russ wondered what torment the wolf was enduring.

From what he'd been able to see of the trap it was a number four jump trap and the jaws had him just above the pad. He wouldn't know if the foot was broken until the trap came off — if he ever got it off.

Now the important thing was to move, to put distance between them and the calf carcass.

When the wolf loomed whitely in the clearing, Russ sat up. "Pretty terrible, Gray? Why don't you let me take it off?" He moved toward the animal but the wolf backed off.

"Okay. Okay. But we can't stay here. They'd have us in a minute."

The boy got to his feet and started toward the railroad. A slice of moon had come into the sky and it added a little light now that the clouds were gone. And so they walked — a frightened, heartsick boy, and a wolf limping on three legs and dragging a six-foot length of chain through all manner of obstacles.

12

AT NOON, Russ turned on the radio to get the news. He got the Clintonville station. The first item confirmed his suspicions. The announcer said:

"The wolf hunt which began in the Kettle Moraine Forest of southeastern Wisconsin has shifted to the Near North. Abe Forsythe, Tigerton farmer, claims a wolf killed a yearling calf and then dragged off a trap set to catch it.

"No dog could have done it," a sheriff's deputy said, quoting Forsythe.

"White hairs, obviously wolf hairs, and tracks larger than a man's hand indicate almost certainly the animal is the white wolf thought to have killed a boy, Russet Clagg of Eagle, after escaping from a kennel in that area.

"Authorities had already been in agreement that the wolf was no longer in southeastern Wisconsin. 'He's gone north,' a sheriff said.

"Local authorities have asked everyone to be on the alert for the animal. Meanwhile, a posse led by trailing dogs has been taken to the sight of the calf kill to see if they can bring the wolf to bay.

"The sheriff's office also issued a warning that all dogs be tied or kenneled and that children not be permitted out after dark.

"Now to the war. Forty-eight enemy soldiers were . . ."

Russ turned the radio off. This time they were in trouble. In the hours before daylight, they had come less than two torturous miles. Hounds would be on them in a matter of minutes, once they got the line and started running it.

Daylight had caught them out in the open, so Russ had crossed fields to where brush and trees hemmed in a meandering creek. But they couldn't stay there. They had no alternative except to move and hope to get far enough out ahead of the hounds to keep from being run down while it was still light.

But, even under cover of darkness, Russ could see no hope for them. If the wolf could be relieved of the trap they might stand a chance, but this way . . .

"Come on, Gray. We have to move."

The boy got up and started upstream along the creek. The wolf, on three legs and with the heavy trap and chain weighing him down, followed.

Progress was slow. Russ figured they hadn't made more than a mile the first hour. Still he hadn't heard the hounds, and his ears and every tingling nerve end was tuned for the first sound of their baying.

Another mile and the wolf lay flat. Foam flecked his muzzle. His eyes had reddened. The usually glistening nose was dry and cracked. His coat looked lifeless and was streaked with blood from the foot, and dirt, and burrs.

Russ looked at his watch. It was obvious they must have brought the dogs in from some distance. Otherwise they would have long been on the trail. It was already three o'clock. There would still be a couple hours before evening began lowering the shades on this terrible day.

He was suffering as much as the wolf. Every step was agony because he knew how much the animal must be enduring.

"People!" The word exploded from the boy. If they would only listen, try to understand. If he could only walk out and explain how the wolf was too frightened of people to harm them. But, *who* would listen? *Who* would help them?

He gave the wolf fifteen minutes and then he was back up and moving again. "Come on, Gray," he urged, "your life depends on it."

The creek was growing smaller and smaller until it dwindled to a trickle. Where it entered a wide area of low brush and glistening white birch it was small enough to step across. Once under the cover of the trees, the boy lay on the creek edge drinking and running water over his face. Downstream, the wolf had gotten right into the water so the trapped foot was submerged.

It was while they were resting that the first faint sound which he had been dreading came drifting to them on the southerly breeze.

"Well, here they come, Gray," the boy said.

But it wasn't necessary to tell the wolf.

Gray knew. He had probably heard them long before Russ had. But now that the boy spoke of it, his ears went flat and his ruff bristled.

"You can't fight them, Gray. With that trap on your leg they'd kill you in minutes."

Russ got up and followed on the creek. The wolf, head hanging, hobbled slowly along behind.

Well, we can walk in the water, Russ thought and stepped into the shallow, narrow creek. But Gray remained on land.

"Let's spread ourselves around a little," the boy said to the wolf. "Maybe it will slow them down."

He circled then and circled again, always coming back to the creek until he had laid a half-dozen scent lines off at varying angles, and always turning back on themselves.

"That should help," the boy said. "And now we've got to move."

The baying of the hounds was clear enough so that Russ could distinguish at least four voices. One dog ran with a sharp chopping bark. Two had deep bass bellows, and they would probably be slow but deadly accurate and obstinate trailers. The fourth was a squealer, probably a feisty dog with something other than hound in his bloodlines.

He might, he thought, catch the dogs one at a time and perhaps tether them before the men came up. Hounds weren't fighters. They'd come to a man. Then he and Gray could gain a little more time while the men came up to turn the dogs back to the trail.

It was obvious Gray was about to collapse. The only thing which kept him going was the beat of the dog voices hammering into his wild brain like a death knell. So he kept going and even increased his pace, hobbling along on courage alone.

The creek narrowed until it was less than a foot across and, abruptly then, they came through the trees to the base of a large beaver dam.

Water trickled through the brush, log, and mud structure, but it was a living dam on which the beaver had been working as recently as the previous night judging by the fresh cuttings.

Russ climbed up and around the dam and there, spreading out behind it, were acres of water from which cropped small alder islands. The wolf had waited at the bottom of the dam, as though the four-foot climb was something he just couldn't accomplish.

"Come on, Gray! Here's where we make our stand!"

Slowly, the wolf clawed up the side of the

embankment. When he got up Russ slipped into knee-deep water and began wading. The wolf waited until the boy was nearly out of sight and then entered the water and floundered along behind.

Russ went to what he judged was the exact center of the beaver pond and guessed he had water on all sides, for a distance of perhaps a couple hundred yards. Then, he stamped himself a place on an alder island, which was no island at all, only bushes protruding up out of the water, and when the muck beneath his feet felt solid, he leaned against a small tree to catch his breath.

The wolf came up and, where beavers had felled a poplar, he got his forepaws up over the log and, with his chin down to rest his head, stood with his hind paws on the pond bottom.

Russ heard the querulous and tentative barking of the dogs and knew they had come to the place where they'd laid the false trails.

"Work your darn heads off!" He was terribly angry. What had the wolf done to deserve this?

"We'll make it yet," he said to Gray. But the wolf was beyond responding to his voice. He lay across the log with his eyes closed, and Russ had the feeling he might be dying.

"Gray!" he shouted at the wolf, and the animal opened his eyes and lifted his ears. "You scared me. Don't die on me now!"

Above the boy and the wolf the slanting rays of the setting sun had put a pale, golden light among the treetops. In a half-hour the beavers would be out working because the shadows would be closing in.

Night couldn't come too soon for the boy. His courage was fast draining away. The long trek with its innumerable hazards was at last taking its toll. Strong as he was physically, he knew now as he stood there in the icy water that when hope went, so did the will to go on.

Now there were shadows on the water, and Russ knew if they could keep the dogs off for a half-hour it would be dark. With evening also came a calm, so their scent line wouldn't be carried ashore on a wind.

He hoped the hounds wouldn't enter the water. He didn't believe they would. They disliked swimming. There would be no scent line to entice them. So, instead, they would probably circle the pond trying to find where the wolf had left it.

Mostly, at the moment, he worried that Gray might die right there with only his head and shoulders above water. He knew there was an endurance point beyond which animals couldn't go without passing into shock. When they came to that point they succumbed quickly.

He'd seen it often enough. Mink in a trap. Deer run by dogs. Bird in a net. Fish in a weir. Rabbit held by the owl's talons. One moment vivaciously alive, the next instantly dead. It was one of the oddities of the animal world that these wild ones, still apparently with reserves of strength, should suddenly collapse and die. Russ hoped it wouldn't happen to the wolf.

The dogs were so close now their yammering seemed to be coming from every direction at once. There, in the usually silent and almost holy sanctuary which a beaver pond can be, the near hysterical baying was a desecration. Gray quivered visibly at the onslaught of sound.

"Easy, Gray. Easy." The boy tried to console the wolf, though he knew the animal was beyond consolation.

Russ could hear the dogs clambering up the dam embankment and then, where the trail ended at the water's edge, there were barks of consternation.

As he had thought, the pack began to circle the pond methodically, searching to discover at what point the wolf had left the water. It was while the dogs were snuffling noisily along the far end of the pond that he heard voices.

The men came to the water's edge, and a searchlight began stabbing out across the pond. Russ pushed hard against the tree. Gray lay like dead.

"The critter crossed here, but the dogs will pick him up," a voice said.

"Well, we might as well make ourselves comfortable while we're waiting," another voice said.

Russ heard the men go back down off the dam and heard them circling through the trees below it. Shortly, he saw the bright light of a fire they'd built and heard their laughter, as they sat waiting for the dogs to announce that they'd found the trail and were lining out again.

The dogs frantically circled the pond twice searching for scent. Then they went to the fire. Russ could tell from the tone of the men's voices that they were disappointed, though he could not hear what they said.

Then, the fire went out. There was a crackling of brush and quickly then no sound at all. Almost at once a beaver was out working and, by the light of the stars, Russ could see the rippling V as the animal swam toward the poplars to get on with the job of cutting and storing food for the winter.

"They're gone, Gray. They're gone." It was a prayer of thanksgiving for once again having been spared.

The boy started away from the alders sloshing through the water on legs reluctant to respond. In a little while he could feel the life come back into them, and then he stopped because he hadn't heard Gray.

He whistled softly and listened, but there was no sound from the wolf. It hit him hard that maybe Gray was dead. He started back and, in his haste, tried to run and went over on his face.

He got up dripping and angry at himself for having lost control.

"Gray? Gray!" He whistled again, but there was nothing. Swinging his pack around off his back he moved to a tree and hung it on a low branch. Then he felt inside until his hand was on the small flashlight.

Snapping the light on, he moved toward the wolf. He still hung on the log with his eyes closed, ears flat, and the boy couldn't tell if he was alive or dead.

"Gray? Gray?" He spoke softly. There was no response from the wolf.

But how could he hang there if he was

dead? Russ moved closer and put the beam of light right into the animal's eyes. He saw a flicker.

At least the wolf was still alive, and right there in front of him on the log was the paw with the trap and if ever there was a time it was now.

"Easy, Gray. Easy. I'm not going to hurt you. . . ."

The boy kept talking as he walked through the water until he was close enough to touch the wolf.

The trap was a large one. It would take all his strength, yet he had to be fast for if the wolf started struggling and slipped off the log he'd likely not be able to keep his head above water.

He put the flashlight into his hunting jacket pocket. Then he waited for his eyes to adjust. When he could see the trap spring he leaned forward and slowly put both hands on it. Then, leaning with all his weight, he depressed the spring and the jaws fell away from the paw. It took all his strength to hold the spring down while he slowly slipped the trap away from the paw to let it fall into the water.

The wolf never moved.

"It's off, Gray. It's off," Russ said jubilantly. But trap or no trap, the boy knew they still had troubles. Gray would not respond.

"Gray! Gray! The trap is off!" Then he felt foolish because, of course, the wolf couldn't understand.

Taking water in his cupped hands he let it flow over the wolf's head. Three times he wetted the wolf down, and then he saw the eyes come open. Backing away slowly, he went to his pack and took out a tin of meat. He cut it open with his knife and, taking the fist-sized piece of meat, walked back to hold it in front of the wolf's nose.

The animal's ears came forward.

"Eat it, Gray. Eat it!"

Saliva began to appear on the wolf's flews, but he did not open his jaws. Gently Russ forced the meat against the wolf's muzzle. The animal lifted his head a little and then he took the meat. As though too weak to chew, he gulped it down.

There were two cans of meat left. Russ cut both open. He fed them to the wolf. Then he poured more water over the wolf's head and waited. Gradually life flowed back into the animal. The eyes came open. The ears came erect. Russ stepped back.

"We've got to get out of here," he said.

Then he turned and started away. He took the pack from the limb and got into it. He walked twenty feet and waited. Nothing. He walked another ten steps and, stopping, whistled softly.

He heard the wolf sloshing through the water.

Slowly then they came to the pond's edge and to dry land, and under the stars a bedraggled wolf on three legs followed a weary, shivering boy north.

13

THEY WERE in a thick stand of brush willow just off the railroad right-of-way when, at seven o'clock, Russ turned on the news. It was the Clintonville station and, once again, the wolf was the first item on the morning report:

"Hound-dog men plan to take their packs out this morning to resume trailing at the beaver dam north of here where the wolf gave them the slip under the cover of darkness last night. Hunters were confident that today would see the end of . . ."

Russ didn't listen to the rest. He turned the radio off. "Gray, we've got to keep moving," he said, getting to his feet.

They had walked all night, but it had been slow going. The wolf had tired fast and they had been forced to rest often. Russ estimated they had come eight, maybe ten miles. But he had been sure to leave a twisting, tortuous trail — walking in water every chance they got, backtracking often, circling so there'd be scent lines going off at many tangents.

Still, he knew they had to risk traveling during daylight to shake free of the hounds. They were north of Tigerton, and he meant to try to get around Wittenberg before dark.

He knew the risk he was taking, but he also knew that the greatest danger was in staying put, hiding out, and having the dogs find them. *And they would* — he knew it for a certainty — no matter how complex the trail, no matter what tricks he tried. In the end, unless they traveled, there would be an end to the trail, a time for reckoning and the fight for survival. Since the wolf was not strong enough to fight there was nothing to do except put enough distance between themselves and the dogs, so they couldn't be caught.

Gray was considerably revived now that the impediment of the trap had been removed and there were no hounds baying in the distance. Animals, if vulnerable to shock, also had great powers of recuperation.

At least they would have one thing going for them. No one would expect to see the wolf walking in the company of a boy. He, Russ, was supposed to be dead and his body moldering somewhere to the south in that slash of forest which was the Kettle Moraine. So, if they were sighted, people might pass Gray off for a big, white dog.

Anyway, they had to chance it, so Russ went to the railroad and they headed north again. Gray, still on three legs, limped along through the weeds off to the side. His head was low and his tongue lolling, but he kept pace with the boy.

Within sight of Wittenberg, the pair stopped when a cottontail dashed across the rails and ducked into a stone fence. Russ went over and piling off the stones came down to where the rabbit was crouched. The cottontail's ears were flat and the eternally twitching nose missed a beat when he made a grab and had the animal. With the heel of his hand he struck it a blow behind the neck and then, to make it easy for the wolf, skinned it out even before it had stopped kicking. Then he threw it to the wolf.

Gray dropped to his belly and ate ravenously. When the carcass was gone, the boy took the last of the food from the pack. There were five candy bars.

"Let's go," he said to the wolf, and now they struck off down a town-line road to swing around Wittenberg.

One car passed them and the driver slowed on seeing the pair, but obviously thinking he was looking at a boy and his dog, picked up speed again.

A quarter-mile down the road and they took to the fields to go around the town. Gray was moving well. Sometimes he even tried his paw, and though it appeared no bones were broken, it was obvious all the tendons had been severed and he'd walk splayfooted for the rest of his life.

Soon as they were north of Wittenberg, Russ cut back to the tracks. It was easier traveling. There were no fences and chances of meeting anyone were relatively scarce.

When he heard a noon fire whistle, he pulled off and dropped in the weeds to rest. Turning on the radio he listened. Once again the wolf was the first item:

"A report just in confirms that hounds have once again picked up the trail of the wolf at the beaver pond where they lost it the previous night. Hound-dog men are confident they will have put the wolf at bay before the day is over. More than a hundred men have joined . . ."

Russ snapped the radio off.

"They're in for a surprise," Russ told the wolf. "What they don't know is that I'm masterminding this escape. By the time they untangle our trail, we're going to be long gone."

He took out a candy bar and ate it. Then he got to his feet and the pair moved north.

All day they walked without incident. Three times they detoured to avoid hunting parties, but the men and boys obviously thought the boy and the white dog were also hunting. They bypassed the tiny village of Eland and just at dusk went around Birnamwood. Then, as the sun was setting, they pulled off the right-of-way into a thick stand of pine and, lying down, both slept.

The stars were bright when Russ awakened. He looked at his watch. It was eleven o'clock. When his eyes began to adjust to the night he looked over and saw Gray watching him.

"Let's walk," he said to the wolf.

Striding back out to the cinder embankment, they walked and didn't stop until day dawned and they could see the outskirts of Antigo.

"We'll sleep today," Russ announced, and they went down into a swamp studded with big spruce, and finding a hummock of higher ground near the heart of it, they made themselves beds of dry grass and slept soundly all day.

When they awakened that evening Russ felt that at last they had made it. They were on the fringe of the great forests which cover northern Wisconsin. He turned on the radio for the six o'clock news and got the Antigo station. There was no mention of the wolf hunt.

"We've lost them for sure, and we've lost them for good," he said.

Yet, he had hardly gotten the words out when from faraway came the thin yammering of a hound, and he couldn't believe it was one which might be following *them*, but perhaps hunting some other creature.

But the tolling came closer, and then, with night sneaking darkly around them from out the swamp pockets, Russ was convinced the dog was on their trail.

"Well, how do we shake that hound?" Russ asked, turning to the wolf.

Gray was looking south, and his ears were flat and his hair bristling.

Russ was reluctant to go around Antigo with a dog on their trail. What's more, he had planned on entering the town for provisions.

If the hound got close enough, Gray would have to try to kill it. Between them, he knew they could do it. But he didn't want that to happen, not unless it was absolutely necessary. When Gray had killed the bloodhound in the Kettle Moraine Forest, Russ hadn't been able to prevent it. But perhaps he could prevent another killing.

But how? Divert the dog to the trail of some other animal? Impossible. Good hounds were known to follow a coyote right through a deeryard or a farmyard hanging doggedly to the scent line they'd been set down on, no matter what multitude of other odors intervened.

Perhaps if they took to a lake. But how? And where?

The boy could think of only one strategy. Instead of heading north and away from the bawling, which was now becoming louder and more insistent, he headed straight toward the dog.

Gray followed along a little way and then sat to watch. He wanted no unnecessary confrontation.

"Okay, Gray. You stay. You'll only be in the way." Rummaging through his pack he brought out the length of rope. Then he put the pack down for the wolf to mark on and stay by.

Russ hit the tracks quickly and headed south. The dog was so close he sometimes thought he could hear the dry weeds breaking as he plowed along. The baying was like the steady snarl of a buzz saw which comes to a crescendo in the heart of a log and then dies away as the cut is made, only to start the ripping sound all over again.

The boy didn't see the dog until he was almost on him. Then the white markings stood out against the tan coat, and Russ walked down to meet him.

Russ called tentatively: "Here, boy. Here."

The baying stopped, and the long-eared hound came cautiously forward.

"Good dog. Good dog."

The hound wagged his tail. Russ went slowly forward, with the hand holding the rope behind his back and the other hand extended.

"I won't hurt you, fella. That's a nice dog."

Now the hound wriggled ecstatically. There was little doubt but that he had enough and was only too glad to be picked up. It was the law of the trailing dog that he might be excused by a man from further pursuing his prey, but he could, under no circumstances, excuse himself — not if he was a good hound with tenacity bred through true to the bone.

Russ had no trouble slipping the rope beneath the hound's collar, in fact the dog seemed to welcome it. Once the rope was on, Russ knelt beside the animal.

The hound's pads were bleeding and the end of its tail was whipped bloody and bare from threshing it through briars. Foam flecked his chest, and the dog's ribs showed through the taut hide like branches of a bush. There was an identity disk on the red collar. Russ turned it to the light of the stars and by squinting could read: "Buzz Saw. Return to Paul Merkle, Marion, Wis. Reward."

Well, he might have known. There wasn't a dog man in the Middle West hadn't heard of Merkle's hounds, and particularly of Buzz Saw. Sport pages had often chronicled the dog's field trial wins, and dog men had come from all parts of the country to listen to him run coyotes along the Stockbridge Indian reservation country. That explained why they hadn't been able to shake the hound, and now he was doubly glad it hadn't been necessary to try to kill him.

But, now that he had the dog, what was he going to do with him? To take him along was out of the question. Buzz Saw would never tolerate the wolf, and Gray undoubtedly would not put up with the dog. To tie him to a fence post was out of the question. That would mean an excruciatingly slow death from thirst and starvation.

No, he had to get the dog to such a place as he'd surely be found and returned to Merkle.

A quarter-mile away were lights of a farmhouse. He headed across the fields with the dog walking contentedly at heel.

As he approached the buildings, a farm dog sounded the alarm. Russ dropped to the ground waiting for the dog to quiet down. When the barking stopped he proceeded again. He was within a hundred feet of the farm driveway when the dog started up again.

This time he didn't wait, but ran forward to the mail box and quickly tied his end of the rope to the post. Then he ran for the cover of a hedgerow and followed it in the direction of the tracks.

Behind him the farm dog kept up the clamor. Then he heard a door slam and he heard voices. He dropped to the ground to get his breath. The farm dog stopped barking. He heard exclamations of surprise. They had found the hound. The dog would be home the next day. He waited until all was quiet and then, getting up, went back to the tracks and followed along until he came to the place where Gray was waiting.

"Well, Gray," he said, "that's one we won't have to worry about. Let's hope it's the last."

14

THAT NIGHT he left the wolf and risked going into Antigo for provisions. Before going to the grocery store, he slipped into a restaurant which was also a drug store, and keeping his face averted, stood before a telephone flanked on either side by protecting walls.

His mother answered the call, and when she heard his voice she wept.

"It's okay, Mother," he tried to reassure her.

"I'm sorry, Russ. I'm sorry. It's just that we heard they were on your trail again."

"Well, I've shaken them. I think we're in the clear."

"Are you getting enough to eat?"

"We're getting more than enough," Russ told her.

"How about sleep, and are you keeping warm?"

"We're both fine," Russ said. "Just fine."

Then he talked to his father.

"Well, you're almost there," his father said, and he could detect the pride and satisfaction in his voice.

"Just about," Russ said.

"What about the trap?"

"You heard about it?"

"On the radio," the father said.

"I got it off. No bones broken."

"When are we likely to hear from you again?" the father asked.

"I don't know. It's hard. Likely not until it's over."

"Just be careful."

"I will, Dad. And now I have to go before I attract attention. I'm in a restaurant."

"Good-bye, Russ."

He hung up and went out and the loneliness was a deep throbbing hurt as he walked the windswept streets of the city looking for a small grocery store in which to buy provisions.

Back with the wolf they both feasted. Then

they went around the city and took a spur track which angled east.

More and more the country was taking on a wild look. Towering pines marked forest tracts. Nearly impenetrable spruce thickets came right down to the tracks in low places. Deer went crashing out ahead of them. They heard horned owls.

Midnight, and they came to rails end at Bryant. They had heard no sounds of pursuit, heard no dogs on their trail. So now Russ headed cross-country and within a matter of hours was deep in a great forest.

He stopped at dawn and made camp where a busy little creek made merry little noises as it rolled out of its banks to spread into a small, sparkling lake. He decided it was time to rest and, in waiting, discover if for sure they had shaken the hound-dog men or if, somehow or other, they had found the trail and were again pursuing them.

All day he moved about, alert to every sound. Sometimes he thought he heard a far-off baying. Then there would be nothing, and he knew it was his imagination.

By evening he had settled down and with the sunset came such a stillness as can come only at dusk. Even the wind had come to rest, and it was a bewitching hour for the boy and the wolf sitting near each other on the shores of the forest-bound lake. There was gold high in the sky, and to the west the forest seemed on fire with sunglow.

It seemed at last they had earned a measure of peace, and Russ felt the holiness of the hour which comes like an interlude between today and tomorrow. As they sat, daytime creatures were going to their roosts, dens — their night camps. Nighttime creatures were up and stretching but not yet about.

It was like a time in between as they watched time run out for the day, though it hadn't yet started for the night. Russ wondered if the whole meaning, perhaps even the reason for life, wasn't wrapped up in this eternity when a day beyond the horizon is beginning and this day is ending.

When at last the only light came from the stars in the sky and the stars in the water, the wolf curled up and the boy lay back, and they slept.

For two days they led an idyllic life. Russ swam in the icy waters of the lake and then came to stretch out on the white sand in the sun. And there were no sounds of pursuit, only the lonely cry of a loon still reluctant to go south, the gabbling of a small mallard flock using one of the sloughs, and the croaking of ravens flying their mysterious missions in the forest.

Gradually, he forgot the discomforts of their arduous trek and found comfort in feasting his eyes on the sun diamonds on the water, the strings of cloud pearls in the sky, the hundred gleaming, glowing shades of color in leaves and stones along the shore.

But then, as all things must, their holiday came to an end. Both felt fit, and though hard and lean and whippy as hickory saplings, there were few physical signs to show how many worrisome miles they had come. Gray was putting his injured paw to the ground and, though the toes splayed out flatly, he was walking on it and moving strongly.

"And it's good you are," Russ said, "because we've got a long way to go. Only now, we travel days."

Staying to the forest they traveled northeast until they came to one of Wisconsin's last wild river, the Wolf. Instead of looking for a bridge, they forded the beautiful stream and rested on the east bank.

Late that afternoon they crossed the tracks of another railroad, the Soo Line, and shortly thereafter came to Highway 55. Russ waited until dark before crossing the road, and then he knew that he had arrived when he flashed his light on a sign which read: "Nicolet National Forest."

From here there was little else but forest for a hundred miles north into Michigan. If he stayed off the roads it wasn't likely they'd run into people.

For two more days they walked north, at last cutting across Highway 32 just south of Wabeno. Here he left the wolf by his pack and went into town for provisions. Then they paralleled County Trunk C to the east for fifteen miles before turning north again.

Now if they went true north, there would be no roads other than logging trails and no towns for a good thirty miles. It was the heart of this wild country which Russ considered his destination. Here was the place he had been aiming for ever since that night he had slipped into the warm clothes and walked out of the Kettle Moraine Forest.

The wolf was walking well. He looked thin but slick. And, above all, he seemed to have once again assumed what he considered the lead role, the position of pack boss.

Russ figured to walk a day and a half and then stop — unless they should be so fortunate as to find wolf signs before that time.

There was still supposed to be a small pack of wolves using the forest, according to the Wisconsin Conservation Department Bulletin. Wardens kept an eye on the pack to afford it protection since it is illegal to shoot a timber wolf in Wisconsin. They trailed them mostly in winter, and from the air, so there would be a minimum of human interference. It was this wolf pack which Russ was determined to find.

Early on the second morning, he found the first sign. There were deep gouges in the earth alongside a stump which obviously had been used as a scent post. Gray inspected the sign and bristled. Then his hair went flat, his ears came up, and he whimpered. Then, at the creek, there were wolf tracks.

Russ moved along, however, because the forest around was too dense for his purpose and shortly broke out into a burn that had grown back with new saplings so there was cover high as his belt.

The burn went up a slope and he followed it to a high knoll, and there he dropped his pack. He had a commanding view of the country on all sides. This was the place at which they would wait.

He spread the contents of his pack on the shelter-half and took inventory. He figured there was food for him for five days. The wolf had nearly ten pounds of dog food left, and after that they'd have to forage in the forest.

There was a creek not too far distant and Russ was sure it contained trout. There were many deer, and perhaps with the help of the wolf he might kill one. There were plenty of ruffed grouse flocks on the edge of the burn, and the young birds often sat stupidly watching from a tree limb so a man might knock one down with a good throwing stick.

They'd make out — somehow.

Now to make camp. With the rags he had brought made into ropes he stretched the shelter-half so it was a lean-to. Then he cut brush and heaped it around to help break the force of any wind. He had hardly finished when the first flakes of the first snowstorm of the year sifted down around them.

So he gathered wood and soon had a fire. Any wild wolves would be accustomed to the smell of smoke, because loggers doing selective cutting often burned slash, and the cook fires from some of the Job Corps Camps had acclimated the animals to the odor.

Taking out his radio, he fiddled with the dial until he had a station coming in strong. It was Marinette, some seventy or eighty miles east from where they were. With the music and the fire and food to eat, and the wolf curled off to one side, Russ had his first real feeling of contentment in many days.

They had come a long way — surely more than two hundred miles as the crow is said to fly, and probably fifty or a hundred more than that considering the winding trail they had followed.

They were superbly conditioned. The wolf, having recuperated from his ordeal of the trap, was lean and tough. The boy, pounds thinner, was supple and rawhide hard. They could relax anywhere — swamp or hill, forest or plain — all they needed was food, and for the moment there was plenty of that.

The snowflakes thickened around them, until Russ could hardly see the bottom of the slope where the burn ended and mature timber put up a high wall of thickly needled limbs. It was a peculiar burn, kidney-shaped, and ending where there was still fuel to have fed the fire. Perhaps, Russ thought, it was a man-made burn, a controlled fire to open the thick woods so sharp-tailed grouse, deer, hares, and other animals and birds needing edge areas might survive. The Conservation Department did that kind of burning to create habitat, to bring sprouts of maple and other saplings up to feed wildlife.

As they sat there, the boy with his back to an old fire-blackened stump and the wolf curled among the saplings, a silence came over the clearing so even the sound of chickadees was muffled by the falling snow.

Russ could not help but feel immensely grateful. Pursuit was unlikely now. They could move freely by daylight and in any direction they desired. He guessed there might not be another man within twenty miles of them in any direction, and now that snow was covering their trail, even the most astute hound would find tracking impossible.

But the boy was not about to fool himself. Probably the most difficult maneuver of their entire operation was still ahead. Intercepting a wolf pack which might conceivably travel sixty miles in a single night was like throwing a dart in the dark and hoping to hit the target.

Only Russ didn't figure on going to the wolves. He was going to let the wolves come to him.

At the moment he wasn't going to worry about it, but only luxuriate in the solitude and warmth of the fire. He even treated himself to a banquet, and setting several tins of meat near the coals so they'd become warm, he cut a forked sapling and toasted bread. It would be the first hot food in a long, long time.

The hot food put a glow in him, and, feeling strong and sure of himself, he got up and started down the slope through the snow, with the wolf coursing out ahead trying the air with his jet-black nose to see what enemy or friend might be beyond, among the trees.

They went as far as the creek. Russ laid flat and drank, and the wolf lapped water too. Then they sat until four trout came out from beneath a bank and, arrowing into the current, took feeding positions just below a riffle which flowed across jewel-bright pebbles.

At intervals the fish would forget there was no flies hatching and rise to the snowflakes which put rings on the water before melting. A muskrat put its whiskered nose and bead-black eyes out of a bankside tunnel and, seeing or scenting nothing, shoved out into the current to cross the creek.

Gray's ears came up and then went flat. He crouched low and when the rodent was a few feet from the bank he leaped forward and, before the muskrat had a chance to dive, he had it between his jaws. The naked tail jerked spasmodically and then hung limp.

"Good going, Gray," the boy said. "You'll make it, but I never thought you wouldn't."

The boy got up and started back toward the clearing. Gray followed with the muskrat between his jaws, and the snowflakes melted on the shiny mahogany hide and fell in drops of water to the snow-covered ground.

The tracks they had made in coming to the creek were already covered, so they made a new trail up through the wealth of whip-like saplings, and, coming to their camp, Russ stirred up the fire and added wood. It caught and lifted in a brilliant blaze of brightness.

Russ brushed snow from the stump and put his back to it. Gray lay off to one side, and, while Russ ate a candy bar, the wolf ate the muskrat.

Now that the time for them to part was approaching, Russ discovered it was going to be harder than he had thought. Down through the years, and especially during their arduous trek north, the wolf had come to mean more to him than he would have been willing to admit.

Now the wolf was watching him with a

puzzled look wrinkling his eyes. He turned his head inquiringly from side to side and then whined softly, and Russ wondered, as he often had before, if animals were capable of sensing a human's moods.

"Gray, Gray," he said softly. "You going to be able to make it?"

Again the wolf whined softly, and then the huge animal got to his feet and, walking through the deep snow, came right up to him and, without hesitation, put his broad head across his legs, into his lap.

Amazed, Russ rubbed the wolf's ruff. He scratched gently behind his ears, between his eyes, and then when the boy's fingers no longer moved through the wolf's coat, Gray lifted his head and went back to his place.

Maybe, just maybe it had been good-bye.

15

DURING THE NIGHT the snow stopped falling, and the morning sun made every pine and spruce a glistening pinnacle of white. With the wolf leading the way, they made separate thrusts in all directions, searching for wolf sign.

In the afternoon Russ built a trap for trout, like the stone weirs which Indians had built and could still be seen along the Crawfish River near his home. He figured it would work because the brookies, fall spawners, would be moving upstream to lay their golden eggs in white rock nests.

And it did work. Three brookies entered the narrow mouth of the trap and then, finding a rock dam blocking further progress, they turned to go back. But, as intended, they took blind leads and ended up in blind rock alleys and were caught.

They were brilliant, satiny fish, almost too beautiful to kill. Bright blue and red spots gave them a jewel-studded appearance and Russ sat admiring them before breaking their necks. Then he gave one to the wolf, and he took the other two back to camp and splitting them on sticks roasted them until they were brown, crisp, and crackling.

What a life! Russ would have had it go on like that forever, but he was no fool, and knew the winter woods for what it was — a killer for the man with no permanent shelter nor an adequate food supply.

But he meant to enjoy it while he could. The huge clearing in which they were camped was like an island, a little world apart in that vast sprawl of trees. It was the place they came back to every night after trudging through the snow looking for wolf sign and food.

Deer used the burn, and Russ had hoped Gray would try to kill one, but though the wolf became excited each time he crossed a fresh deer trail, he made no effort to follow.

Porcupines were plentiful, and Russ knew that as a last resort they could surely survive on their flesh. But right now he wanted no part of them, because he was afraid the wolf might come by a face full of quills and he knew he'd never get close enough to Gray to pull them out.

Twice they had eaten ruffed grouse. One young bird which had refused to move from its low perch in a poplar was knocked out of the tree with a stick. Another bird was caught when Russ saw it dive into a snowbank just before dark, to camp there warm and secure for the night.

They found a black bear in its den beneath the roots of a deadfall. Gray had retreated at the smell of the bear, but Russ poked deep enough to get a glimpse of hide. Then, when the bear sleepily lifted its head to see what manner of creature had the temerity to invade its place of hibernation, the boy quickly backed off. He wanted no quarrel with a bear.

There had been only one anxious moment. While hiding in a stand of young spruce to see if any of a grouse flock budding in some birch might dive into the snow for the night, Russ had waited too long and had to find his way back to the clearing in the dark.

In trying to come to their camp, he had miscalculated and went south of the clearing and on into the forest.

Three times he had made stabs in the dark to come to the burn, but each time he had missed. It was nearly midnight before he made himself go all the way back to the creek and follow its winding route to where he could tell from the topography that he was just below the clearing.

But mostly the days were without crisis, and then they came to the fifth evening and the sun went down looking red and angry as an infected boil. That night the cold came. Russ was up at midnight building up the fire, but no matter how close he crouched, some portion of his body was always cold.

Long before dawn he ran out of wood, and knowing it would be useless to go down among the trees in the dark to search for more, he walked until the daylight came in dirty gray streaks across the dark sky. He immediately went for wood and when he'd built up the fire, he let the heat wash across himself. Then he looked to the sky and knew for a certainty that more snow was in the offing.

Now Russ was apprehensive. The food was disappearing. The temperature he was certain was at least ten degrees below zero. And a storm was building.

Well, wood was the first worry. All morning he hauled wood up the slope until he had a sizable pile — enough, he hoped, to last through the night.

But even when he built the fire up, he could not recapture the fine feeling he had had. He was depressed. The thought of being driven back out of the forest by cold, snow, and lack of food dogged his thoughts.

He couldn't, he wouldn't let it happen! He had come this far against tremendous odds. He couldn't give up now.

"Gray, why don't you just take off? This is your place, your home. Why don't you leave me so I can go home too?" He had hoped but never really believed the wolf would leave on his own accord, and now he was certain that he wouldn't.

The snow began to fall about the middle of the afternoon. It came softly at first, in huge, widely scattered flakes. Gradually the storm built then, until the clearing was a whiteness and their world was narrowed down to a tight circle of brightness which marked the fire.

Russ divided the last of the food and they ate. Then he stood watching the flakes sizzle out in the flames, wondering what next to do.

With the snow came such intense cold, Russ was forced to build a second fire so he could be between two areas of warmth. Gray had curled up and was soon covered. The pair of fires helped, and Russ dozed.

He had no idea how long he'd been sleeping when he was jolted upright by the sound he'd been waiting to hear. He looked over to where Gray had been sleeping and the wolf was sitting up and staring out through the snow, into the darkness.

Then it came again, a wild howl winging up to them from the forest below — the cry of a wolf. Long after the last plaintive tremolo had been smothered by the heavily falling snow, Gray lifted his muzzle and answered the call.

The boy felt shivers running up and down his back, and he felt the little hairs on his body lift as he leaned forward, almost like a wolf himself, straining against the night to know what wolf was down there where the trees stood.

But the wolf in the woods did not howl again, and Russ wondered if the fires had frightened it, though he didn't dare extinguish them or he would surely freeze to death there on the knoll.

After the exchange of greetings, the night seemed forever, and then when dawn came it was such a gradual lighting of the area around, the boy hardly noticed. But soon as it was light, the flakes began to thin out and then, except for intermittent spits of snow, the storm ended.

There was two feet of snow on the slope, and Russ knew winter was on its way to locking the door and, if he wanted to get out, it would have to be soon.

He planned that morning to look for wolf tracks and to hunt hares in the deep snow, because he couldn't think of any other way of getting food. He was about to leave the fire when movement at the edge of the trees took his attention. He sank slowly to a kneeling position and looked over at Gray.

The wolf had not only seen the movement, but he had scented something and was vibrant with excitement.

Boy and wolf remained immobile, and then like shadows among the trees, they caught glimpses of gray. Almost as though conjured out of the cold winter air there suddenly appeared a wolf. The boy didn't see it walk from the woods. It was just suddenly there.

Gray whined. Then a second wolf came into the clearing. Gray whined again. Then at once, more wolves came out from among the trees until there were seven.

Gray lifted to his feet and started down

the slope toward them. Halfway he stopped and looked back at the boy. Then he whined, turned his head, and walked again.

One of the pack of seven wolves came forward. Gray moved closer. So did the wild one. Then when they were a dozen feet apart they stood testing the air.

Now the other six wild ones moved forward until they were standing in a half-circle around Gray and the wolf who was obviously leader of the pack. They were all dark, almost black, and they stood out in vivid contrast to the white wolf they were inspecting.

Russ appreciated that he was seeing a dramatic happening, a primitive confrontation. In the background were the towering pines, their boughs with scarves of snow. And there in the clearing, motionless as in a tableau, stood the wolves, all eyeing the strange one.

Sometimes, as he watched, Russ found it difficult to believe that they were real live wolves and not the product of some artist's brush. Then suddenly the tableau broke, and the pack leader began to circle Gray.

He went around and around, stiff-legged and bristling. Gray stood his ground. He never moved. He showed nothing.

Twice around and the pack leader came toward Gray. When they were a couple of feet apart he stopped. Then the hairs of his ruff smoothed out. The pack leader gave a few wags of his tail and Gray responded.

Immediately the wolves which had been in the semicircle broke away, and before Russ could take a deep breath of relief all of them — Gray included — had vanished like mist among the trees.

Still Russ waited, until the cold was biting so deep he had to move. Then he threw on all the wood and, standing as close as he dared, let the heat go deep.

A wolf howled. Russ wondered if it was Gray. The sound seemed to come from far, far away.

It was over, and he had made it happen. Now he could go. Walk out of the woods. Hike to Wabeno. Go to a telephone. Dial and then, when he heard his father's voice, say: "He made it. You can come. I'm at Wabeno."